A SCHOOL IS BORN...

Old records of Chester Preparative Meeting of Friends show that the ground for the old stone schoolhouse was bought by the Elders and Overseers of the Meeting from Ephraim Haines in 12th month 1781. The lot contained 2 acres, 3 roods, and 23 perches of land, and the amount paid for it, including fencing, was 112 pounds, 3 shillings, and 2 pence, Pennsylvania and New Jersey currency. The cost of the stone building was 264 pounds, and since a dollar in federal money was equal to 7 shillings and 6 pence, the total expenditure for the school was 1003 and 9/100 dollars. This sum was subscribed by 33 Friends families:

John Collins

Hugh Cowperthwaite

Robert French

John Haines

Edmund Hollinshead

Eleanor Hollinshead

Jacob Hollinshead

Morgan Hollinshead

Joseph Hackney Sr.

John Hunt

Joshua Hunt

Jesse Linch

Samuel Lippincott

Thomas Lippincott

John Matlack

Reuben Matlack

Samuel Matlack

Sarah Matlack on behalf of herself and
    deceased husband George Matlack

William Matlack

William Matlack Jr.

Enoch Roberts & Son

John Roberts

Joseph Roberts

Joshua Roberts

Samuel Roberts Sr.

Samuel Roberts

William Roberts

Richard S. Smith

Anna Stokes

Abraham Warrington

Henry Warrington

John Warrington

Joseph Warrington

Source: 1935 commemorative edition of the *Moorestown News* celebrating the 150th anniversary of Moorestown Friends School.

DOING WELL
and
DOING GOOD

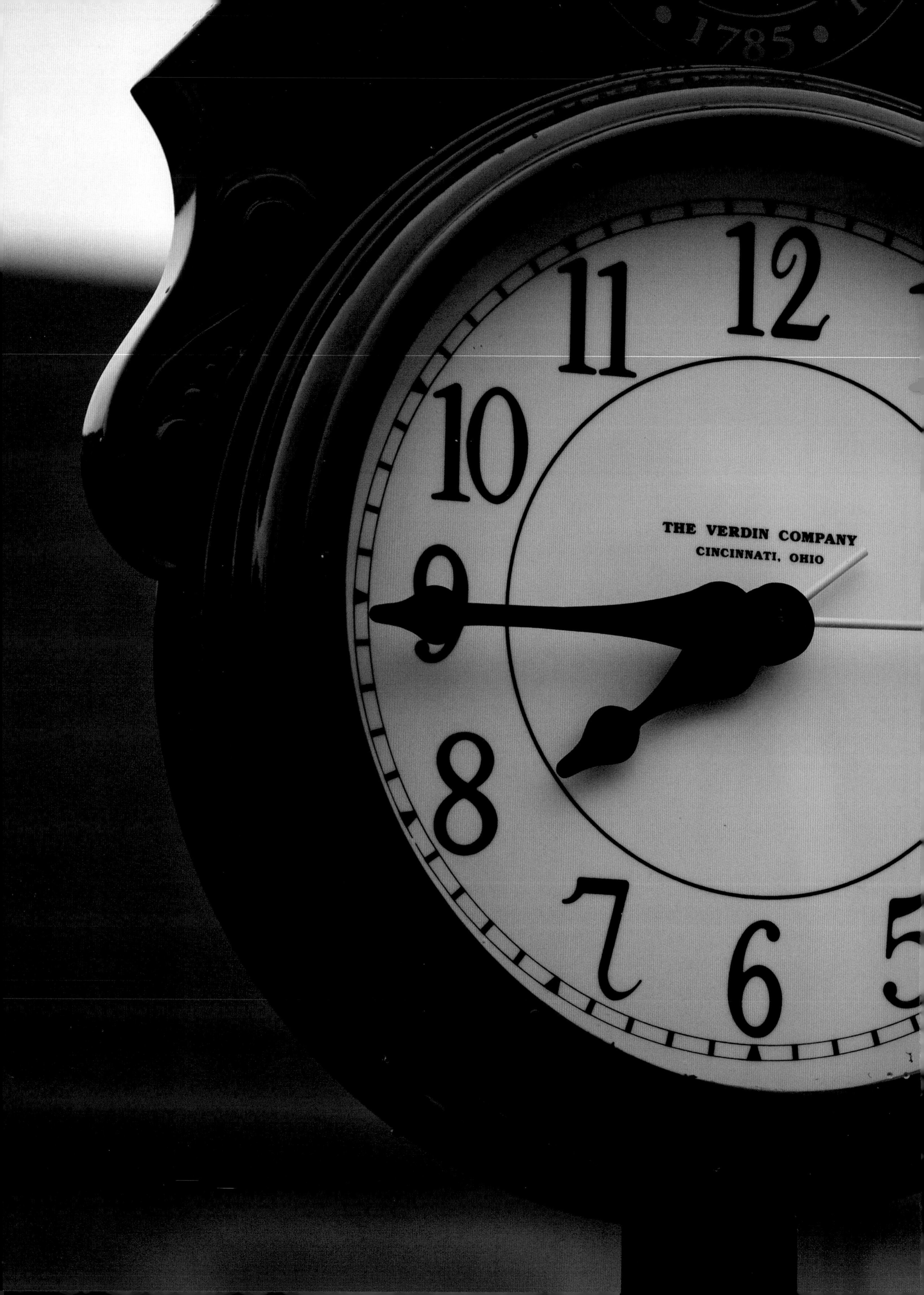
1785
THE VERDIN COMPANY
CINCINNATI, OHIO

DOING WELL
and
DOING GOOD

Moorestown Friends School at 225

MARGARET O. KIRK

DOING WELL
and
DOING GOOD

Editorial Director . . . . Rob Levin

Managing Editor . . . . Sarah E. Fedota

MFS Liaison . . . . Mike Schlotterbeck

Chief Operating Officer . . . . Renée Peyton

Writer . . . . Margaret O. Kirk

Designers . . . . Jill Dible | Laurie Porter

New Photography . . . . Mario Morgado

Copyediting and Indexing . . . . Bob Land

Page 10 photo: William H. Roberts, courtesy of the
Historical Society of Moorestown

Photography by Mario Morgado: Jacket, title page, copyright, contents,
7, 14, 38, 40, 43, 47, 49, 51, 54, 55, 56, 57, 58, 59, 61, 62, 65, 66, 67,
68, 70, 71, 73, 74, 75, 76, 77, 83, 85, 86, 89, 98, 105, 117, 118, 119, 120.

All other photography property of Moorestown Friends School.

ISBN: 978-1-4507-3206-2

MFS | *1785*

Moorestown Friends School
Celebrating 225 years

Copyright 2010 © Moorestown Friends School
110 East Main Street
Moorestown, New Jersey 08057-2922
www.mfriends.org

Book Development by
Bookhouse Group, Inc.
Atlanta, Georgia
www.bookhouse.net

While the contents of this book are correct to the best of our knowledge,
research is a continual process. We encourage anyone who has relevant
information to contact Moorestown Friends School.

CONTENTS

Introduction 7

Chapter 1: Early History from 1785 to 1920 10

Chapter 2: Heads of School from 1920 to 2010:
Eight Leaders Who Build, Grow, and Lead MFS 20

Chapter 3: Quaker Traditions
and Commitment to Diversity 52

Chapter 4: The Educational Core:
A Look at an MFS Education 64

Chapter 5: Teaching and Coaching Icons 78

Chapter 6: Student Traditions, Hallmarks, and Fun 94

Chapter 7: School Committee, Parents, and Alumni 106

Conclusion 116

Appendix
Alumni Association Awards 121
Cum Laude Society 121
School Committee 123

Index 126

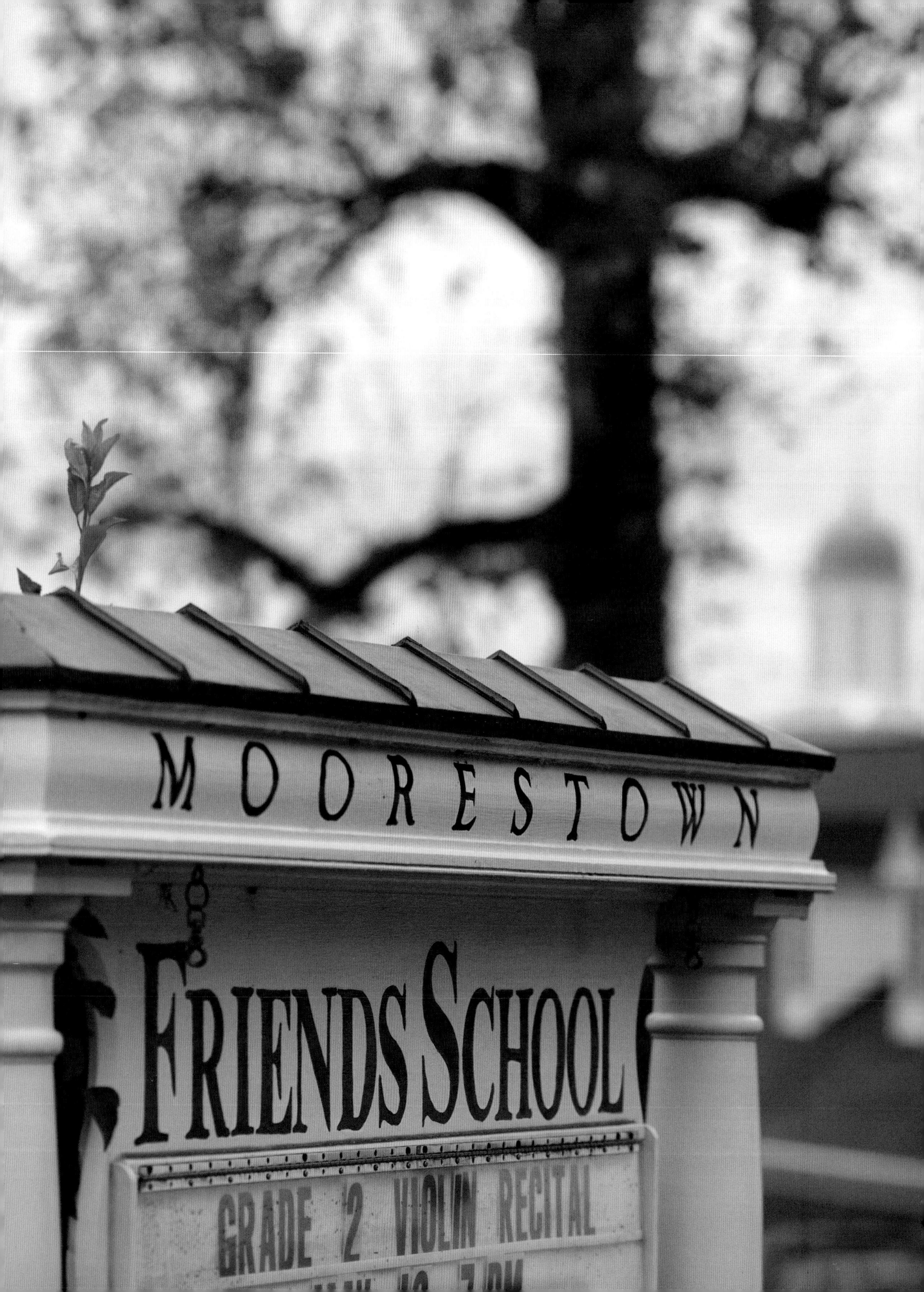
MOORESTOWN
FRIENDS SCHOOL
GRADE 2 VIOLIN RECITAL

INTRODUCTION

It is the first day of classes, the beginning of a new year at Moorestown Friends School. From a campus of buildings both old and new, tucked into a pocket of land that fronts 110 East Main Street, this historic Moorestown, New Jersey, institution appears ready. The traditional sidewalk rainbow is in place for another generation of preschool and prekindergarten students, leading them from the White Building to the Lower School. The Hippo, a cherished outdoor landmark, sports its fresh new coat of back-to-school paint. The scenic Oval sweeps past the athletic fields and leads to the main entrance of the Middle/Upper School, where an electronic message board and old-fashioned bulletin boards already hold details about advisors, class schedules, college visiting, fall musical tryouts, and enticing options for fulfilling service hours. Senior benches claim a prominent hallway spot and suggest an even more imposing tradition. The hallway to the Field House is oddly quiet, though soccer, tennis, cross-country, and field hockey teams have already spent weeks in preseason practice sessions. Rows of shiny lockers line up in three shades of blue, without even a hint of the spectacular decorations that will surface when Spirit Week takes over.

Lower School students follow the rainbow to begin another day.

Stokes Hall, an architectural linchpin between the Lower School and Middle/Upper School, offers a soothing transition between the two buildings, the place where students and teachers alike walk on their way to the noisy, ubiquitous chatter of the Dining Hall Commons or to the

Mist rises off the athletic fields at MFS.

restorative quiet of the historic Moorestown Friends Meeting House.

And that's where you hear it: the soft chimes of the tall case clock in the Stokes Hall lobby, a reproduction of a 200-year-old Hollinshead clock that many students and one determined head of school built in the school's woodshop over the course of several years. It is 8:05 a.m., time for school to begin.

For the rest of this opening day, students at Moorestown Friends School do what students have done every year since the school first opened in 1785. They say good-bye to parents, embrace their friends, and greet teachers. They figure out their schedules and find their classrooms. They observe a moment of silence at the beginning of individual school assemblies, and take part in the Quaker religious service of Meeting for Worship. No matter the grade, every student who passes through Stokes Hall can't help but notice the historical black-and-white photographs from the school's past, hanging on every wall. There's the 1887–1888 faculty photo and a sewing class in 1915. There's a collage of all the campus buildings in 1927, before the high school was built and while Pages Lane still bisected the campus. Frame after frame of graduation portraits and sports teams remind students that they walk in others' footsteps, and one photograph certainly must be everyone's favorite: the endearing kindergarten class from 1933, with students painting, ironing, working with clay, and building with the popular wooden blocks that many former students still remember fondly.

The echoes of history no doubt loom large at Moorestown Friends School. But as the school celebrates its 225th anniversary in 2010–2011 it is clear that the students who attend this independent Quaker school literally move each day beyond the school's history and into classrooms and activities that prepare them for the future. With an emphasis on personal, ethical, and spiritual growth, Moorestown Friends School promotes a tradition of excellence that is best represented by students who, as faculty and staff like to say, "do well and do good." Students here are encouraged to explore the world and their place in it, to lead what the school calls an "Examined Life" that is characterized by dedication to critical thought, openness to the Spirit, ethical development, and resilience. Within these school walls, teachers at every grade level stress independent thinking, with special emphasis on the moral and ethical underpinnings of intellectual inquiry. More often than not, students at Moorestown Friends School hear a teacher ask, "What do *you* think?"

The goal of today's Quaker education is ambitious—one not easily obtained without the support of dedicated students, parents, faculty, staff, alumni, and trustees. But like so much about the venerable institution known as Moorestown Friends School, its goals are not new. Its future is grounded by its past, anchored to the teachings of George Fox, the founder of the Society of Friends who in 1656 challenged his fellow Quakers to live a life of meaning: "Be patterns, be examples in all countries, places, islands, nations, wherever you go. . . . Then you will come to walk cheerfully over the world, answering that of God in every one."

The Upper School hallway is crowded between classes as students chat with classmates.

1

From the original
stone schoolhouse
to the Moorestown
Friends School
campus—the
school's first
135 years.

EARLY HISTORY
FROM 1785 TO 1920

Main Street in downtown Moorestown, perhaps around the turn of the last century,
when the trolley (shown here) ferried riders across town.

CELEBRATING 225 YEARS
OF QUAKER EDUCATION

Early 1900s

In the fall of 1920, on a September day described by Quakers as "Ninth Month 20," the Religious Society of Friends officially opens another Quaker school in Moorestown, New Jersey. The school is, in many respects, new. It has a new name, a new head of school, and a new tan catalogue that is sixteen-pages slim, with the school's new name and its opening year printed in bold italics on the front cover: *Moorestown Friends' School 1920–21.*

But on page seven of the introductory catalogue, Head of School W. Elmer Barrett reveals why Moorestown Friends' School is not really new at all. The school is, rather, the product of two existing Quaker schools that have merged to become one—a consolidated school that will forever trace its beginnings back to 1785, when Quakers in Moorestown opened their first schools:

The consolidation of Friends' High School and Moorestown Friends' Academy under the name of Moorestown Friends' School has recently been accomplished. The Academy building will be used for the Kindergarten and Elementary grades, the High School building for the Junior and Senior High School. The pooling of all the resources of the two schools will enable the committee of management to conduct a much stronger school than either could be alone.

In two different buildings located just a few blocks from each other, Moorestown Friends' School seeks to retain the spiritual and educational essence of both Friends' High School and Moorestown Friends' Academy. The consolidated school reflects the enduring Quaker testimonies of simplicity, peace, integrity, community, equality, and stewardship, and promotes the overarching Quaker belief that there is "that of God in everyone." In the catalogue the school also pledges to "surround the children with those influences that tend to develop in them strength of character which will stand the stress of later years." It emphasizes a rigorous, college preparatory program for young men and women alike. In addition to basic studies in English, arithmetic, and history, the school offers

MEMORY MILESTONE

Miss Helen Wilson, of Chester Avenue near Main Street, also recalls vividly the days she spent as a little girl in the old stone school building. There was no music taught in the Friends' schools of that period. The nearest approach to music was the sing-song form of recitation used by the children in giving the capitals of states and other useful information, and the singing of the alphabet. . . . The younger children droned out their abc's in similar fashion. . . . Old-time schools were noisy places, when study was going on.

—The Moorestown News, *May 8, 1935, commemorating the 150th anniversary of Moorestown Friends School*

Scripture (Bible studies and memorization of passages), nature study (school gardens, field trips, bird walks, soil formation, and germination studies), and art (drawing, color work, weaving, and singing), with Latin and French offered in the upper grades. And with "possession of a convenient and ample athletic field," the school leaders also note the importance of physical activity as "an absolute essential to the best mental development."

From 1785 to 1920, the early history of Moorestown Friends' School includes a charming but rather curious and complicated litany of "twos." Namely, there were *two* early Quaker schools—one stone, one brick, both built in 1785. In 1827, in a dispute over conservative and liberal teachings within the broader Quaker faith, the Moorestown Meeting split into *two* divisions—the Orthodox meeting and the Hicksite meeting. These two meetings then created *two* separate schools—Friends' High and Friends' Academy, that, after 93 years, were reconsolidated to create Moorestown Friends' School that autumn day in 1920.

The Friends' Academy and its student body, probably between 1888 and 1890.

This history obviously unfolds in Moorestown—a rural, bucolic, and predominantly Quaker farming community barely 14 miles across the Delaware River from Philadelphia, Pennsylvania. Originally made up of two villages called Rodmantown and Chestertown, the township was founded in 1682 but didn't become known as Moorestown until the mid-1800s, a tribute to one of the area's largest land and business owners, Thomas Moore. "Practically all of the earliest settlers of the part of New Jersey, which is now Burlington County, were members of the Society of Friends," according to a 150-year history of Moorestown Friends published in 1935. "Their farms dotted the pleasant country-side bordering the Pennsauken and Rancocas Creeks. Their quiet villages grew up along the Indian trails that had become highways. And their Meeting Houses stood at every important crossroads. One of the characteristics of the Society of Friends, from its beginnings in the 17th century, has always been a strong concern for the education of children."

A capsule history of the community, which was established in the late 1600s, is retold on this street sign in downtown Moorestown.

During Colonial times, local families often maintained small Quaker schools in Quaker homes. But by 1779, according to old minutes from the nearby Evesham Monthly Meeting and reported in previous histories, Quakers appointed a committee "for ye regulating of schools," with the recommendation that each particular Monthly Meeting establish a school. Two years later in Moorestown, the Chester Preparative Meeting of Friends bought a piece of land in order to build a schoolhouse on the south side of what was then known as Salem Road or today's Main Street, just a stone's throw from the Moorestown Meeting House, a log structure then located on the north side of the street on the site of the Friends' cemetery. A historical sketch from a Moorestown Friends' Academy yearbook in 1914–1915 tells the story:

MEMORY MILESTONE

In the year 1920, a small and bellowing group met in the Kindergarten room, little realizing in the midst of its howls and yells that it was the first class to enter under a new regime in which the two Friends' schools were merged under the name of "Moorestown Friends' School." We hurled blocks and "troubled deaf Heaven with our bootless cries."

—*The first day of kindergarten at Moorestown Friends School, recalled by seniors in their 1933 yearbook*

Although the records in our possession are rather meager, it appears that on the 27th day of the Twelfth-month, 1781, Ephraim Haines sold and conveyed unto Joshua Roberts and others, Elders and Overseers of Chester Preparative Meeting of Friends, a certain lot or piece of land for the building of a school house thereon—situated on the south side of the present Moorestown street, but then called the "Salem Road" containing two acres, three roods, and twenty-three perches of land. This is the lot on which the original stone building was erected. . . . The cost of the lot including fencing, etc., was 112 pounds, 3 shillings and 6 pence, equaled one dollar in Federal money, the whole cost was 1003 9-100 dollars. It appears to have been completed and occupied for school purposes in 1785.

Often referred to as "the oldest educational establishment in South Jersey," this one-room schoolhouse built of fieldstone was 35 feet long by 25 feet wide. According to newspaper reports, it faced south, away from Main Street and into the

Students work on financial and other useful skills in 1928.

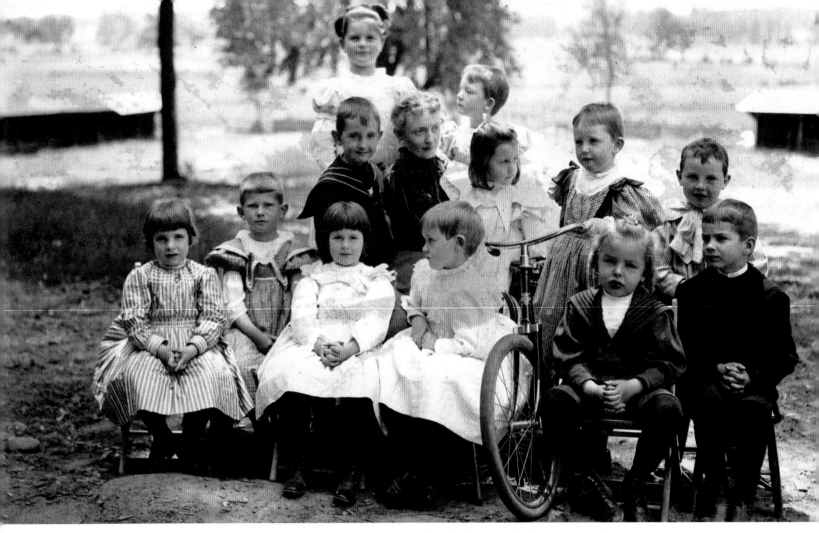

Friends' Academy kindergarten, 1898

soft pitch of the grass-covered valley, and featured a small roofed porch with three wooden steps leading to its front door. Inside there was an aisle, about eight feet wide, running down the middle of the room, with benches on either side. The benches had no backs, and the students leaned on the desks behind them for support. There were no blackboards and no maps—most of the students' work was done on slates and by oral recitation.

In the same year that this first stone schoolhouse opened, the Quaker Meeting decided to build a second school on a lot purchased in 1784 from Job and Ann Cowperthwaite along the western end of Moorestown, near property owned by well-known farmer William Matlack. This school was built of bricks, and it also opened in 1785; some historians argue that the brick schoolhouse actually opened before the stone schoolhouse, but no one disagrees that the land for the stone building was purchased first, in 1781. According to George DeCou's 1929 history, *Moorestown and Her Neighbors*, Moorestown Friends Meeting in 1786 appointed their first committee to "have the care and oversight" of the two schools, a year after they opened. According to later histories,

> The progress of these two schools in Moorestown is reported frequently. . . .
> Sometimes the schools were filled; sometimes the attendance was dis-
> couragingly small. In 1790, action was taken to raise a fund, the interest

from which was to be applied "to the education of such children as belong to the said Meeting . . . whose parents are . . . in low circumstances."

These two early Quaker schools opened decades before public schools existed in New Jersey. The first district school in Moorestown, known as a "Rate Bill" school—which required parents to pay a small sum per day for each child—opened around 1830 at the southeast corner of what became Church and Second streets. Free public schools were not sanctioned in New Jersey until 1871, and not until 1873 did the first public school open in Moorestown.

As the public school system struggled to get established, Quaker schools continued to expand in the Moorestown area. From all accounts, the Orthodox Friends maintained the original stone school. As enrollment grew, the Meeting gradually expanded the building—first, a one-room brick addition, followed by a second story and an impressive new entrance, later enhanced by a two-story addition on the south end

An interesting view of the West Meeting House, built in 1897 by Orthodox Quakers. In 1910 the view was obscured when the elementary school was enlarged to include a gymnasium and library.

The Friends' Academy student body in 1880, dressed in their best clothes, pose in front of the school library.

of the original structure, and then followed by an entirely new front that was soon covered in ivy. In 1878, this expanded school was named Moorestown Friends' Academy. Though it started out as the one-room schoolhouse in 1785, the only visible reference to the original stone school could be found on the west wall of the Friends' Academy, which incorporated stones from the original 1785 structure.

The Hicksite Friends took over the original brick Quaker school in 1827, and used it for the education of Friends until 1872, when Burlington County acquired it for use as a public school. In 1829, the Hicksites also built a frame schoolhouse that became known as Friends' High School on Chester Avenue, close to what is now Second Street. The building was eventually moved north just a bit and replaced by a larger brick structure in 1880. In 1883, Friends' High School, which already served 12 grade levels, expanded to include what many consider the first kindergarten class in Moorestown. In 1891, a young girl named Alice Paul was one of 11 students enrolled in the kindergarten class. Later known as one of the country's leading advocates for women's rights and an American suffragist leader, Alice Paul continued to study at the school, where she excelled both academically and athletically, and graduated at the top of her class of 1901.

For decades, the Hicksites' Friends' High School and the Orthodox Quakers' Friends' Academy "trained many hundreds of young people for college and useful citizenship," according to a school history written in 1935. "Both institutions were staffed by devoted teachers whose influence will long be felt. Their pupils have become leaders in business and the professions, good fathers and mothers."

But the two schools gradually suffered from a lack of students, reflecting what author William H. Kingston III called a gradual decline in the "Quaker numerical presence" during "the course of Moorestown's third century." Though nearly all of the early township settlers were Quaker families, Kingston notes that, by 1880, Quakers made up only 15 percent of the village of Moorestown, a declining trend that continued for decades and clearly had an impact on enrollment in Quaker schools. In 1919, for instance, when tuitions for kindergarten to high school (then called First Class) ranged from $30 a term to $57.50 a term, Friends' Academy had no seniors, only four juniors, no sophomores, and just eight freshmen. During the same year at Friends' High School, where tuition rates ranged from $30 per term for kindergarten to $60 per term for high school juniors and seniors (or Fifth Year and Sixth Year students, as they were called), there were only 16 students in the entire high school.

Working behind the scenes, Quakers in both the Orthodox and Hicksite Meetings negotiated to put 93 years of division behind them and consolidate the two schools, opening as one school in the fall of 1920. The new school with a rich past would have two buildings in two different locations. The former Friends' Academy, located on the original site of the first stone Quaker school, became the home for the lower grades; the former Friends' High School housed the upper grades. But its new name— Moorestown Friends' School—reflected the Quaker belief that the two school communities were ready to move beyond their individual histories and support one school.

Though it long ago dropped the apostrophe in its original name, Moorestown Friends School still exists on the same site where the original stone Quaker school first stood. Its 48-acre campus remains a visible and important anchor in the community where it began, a lasting legacy to not only the one-room stone schoolhouse from 1785 but the two Quaker schools that consolidated in 1920.

A sketch of the original Moorestown Friends' stone schoolhouse in 1785

2

From 1920 to 2010, in tenures that ranged from one to thirty years, eight men led the consolidated Moorestown Friends School.

Heads of School from 1920 to 2010:

Eight Leaders Who Build, Grow, and Lead MFS

The 1923 production of *Cranford*

Celebrating 225 Years
of Quaker Education

1961

From 1920 to 2010, in tenures that ranged from one to 30 years, eight men led the combined Moorestown Friends School. As individuals, they brought talents, quirks, and passion to their mission. As a group, they set the collective tone and direction of the school, dedicated to the Quaker ideals of an academic and spiritual education. The stories of these men document the challenges they faced as each worked to grow a school that developed into one of the outstanding Quaker day schools in the country.

Elmer Barrett initially hesitated before taking the job as the first headmaster at the newly combined Moorestown Friends School in 1920. He accepted the job with one caveat: that he would only serve for five years. By the time he left in 1925, he had laid a solid foundation for his successor.

W. Elmer Barrett: 1920–1925

In 1920, W. Elmer Barrett was described as a "man with a foot in each camp." He was an Orthodox Friend from Philadelphia who had served for 10 years as the headmaster of Friends' Central School, a Philadelphia school run by Hicksite Quakers. Who better than Barrett to lead the newly merged school in Moorestown that combined an Orthodox school with a Hicksite school?

Barrett, however, hesitated. He had recently resigned from Friends' Central due to health problems, and he wanted his next job to be more relaxed, perhaps outdoors. There was no question that being the first headmaster at Moorestown Friends School would be challenging: two aging buildings in two separate locations, plus two sets of faculties, students, and traditions to combine after years of competitive and emotional distance. And even though the two Quaker factions had agreed to combine schools, another three decades would pass before the Orthodox and Hicksite Quakers joined Meetings. The very setting of the new school provided a visual reminder of the lingering Quaker divide because the former Friends' Academy building—now home to Moorestown Friends elementary grades—sat squarely between the Hicksites' 1802 Meeting House and the West Meeting House, built by Orthodox Quakers in 1897 after the 1827 split and barely 200 feet west of the original Meeting.

MEMORY MILESTONE

We brought our sleds to school. There was a slope beginning next to the building and running south to the fields. We would head down the driveway, dodging trees. We could go all the way from Main Street to the present athletic field on one run. It was quite a walk back to the top where we would start all over again.

—*Sam Allen '25, on sledding at recess and after school*

But the School Committee members pushed Barrett to say "yes." They advocated the virtues of their rural township to appeal to Barrett's desire for quieter living. They

From the very beginning, the sciences have been an important part of the MFS academic tradition.

pointed out that he had a clear, uncontested path to the position as Katharine M. Denworth, principal of the former Friends' High School, had retired. Former Friends' Academy principal Alfred L. Deyo and vice principal Martha C. H. Swan had agreed to stay as teachers and assistants in the new high school and elementary school, respectively. Counting Deyo and Swan, 10 of the 17 faculty members in the new school were former teachers at one of the two schools, a factor that seemed to foreshadow a smooth transition.

Barrett finally agreed, with one caveat: he would only be headmaster for five years.

From 1920 to 1925, Barrett skillfully presided over a Quaker school that grew as one from two. He negotiated old rivalries and encouraged new alliances. He moved constantly between both schools, keeping office hours at the high school before 10 a.m. and after 2:15 p.m. and working at the elementary school in between. He oversaw a program that offered "purposeful activity" and "happy freedom" in kindergarten; weekly Meeting for Worship in the West Meeting House, along with the study of Scripture; nature study and bird walks for elementary students as they began to develop "leadership, trustworthiness and consideration for others;" and college preparatory studies in junior and senior high school. The first headmaster also taught math, reflecting the reality that heads of schools rarely performed just one job.

A physical education class takes place on the wooden tennis courts in the 1930s.

"He was great. He was sharp-minded and really kept you on your toes," recalled Sam Allen '25.

Robert Matlack '27, a fifth grader in 1920 and a descendant of one of the original 33 families that started the school, noted that while there may have been some tensions when the two schools combined, there were virtually no discipline problems. "Everything ran smoothly," said Matlack, whose children and grandchildren would one day study here, "and the students respected their teachers."

True to his word, Barrett retired after the 1924–1925 school year. Under his watch, enrollment increased from 232 to 244 students, tuition for 12th grade rose from $160 to $225, and the blue and brown colors of Friends' Academy merged with the red and black of Friends' High School to become the new school colors of red and blue. "Moorestown Friends School has had an honorable past," Barrett said after leaving. "May increasing years bring added strength, high ideals, and the courage to carry out the vision of its founders."

Chester Reagan: 1925–1955

If a person was ever suited to bring strength, high ideals, and courage to a school, that person would be Chester L. Reagan. A scholar, athlete, teacher, coach, husband, father of three, visionary, and Quaker, Reagan was an assistant principal at Friends' Select School in Philadelphia in 1925 when he accepted the offer to lead MFS. He retained the title of headmaster for an extraordinary three decades.

"To understand the school in those days, you need to know more about Chester Reagan," said the late Harrie B. Price III, a teacher and administrator whom Reagan recruited in 1952. "Moorestown Friends was *his* school."

Reagan endeared himself to students from the start. A firm believer in coeducation, he did away with the no-dancing clause at the school (a merger provision that reflected the more conservative Orthodox camp) and allowed both junior and senior proms. In 1926, Reagan literally flipped the schools—sending the lower grades to the former Friends' High School at Second and Chester streets and bringing the older students to the former Academy building at Main and Chester, where the expansive playing fields, the new wooden tennis courts, and an outdoor stage for drama

Chester Reagan, headmaster from 1925 through 1955, was a visionary who indelibly shaped the long-term future of MFS. He hired a generation of memorable teachers, brought the two MFS campuses onto one address, and steered the school from near insolvency to health.

better suited the upper classes. Sports and extracurricular activities, including the first student government and an all-school intramural sports contest known as Red and Blue, began to flourish at the school, and Reagan rarely missed an opportunity to cheer for the teams. There was a new school seal, the first school song, and a new lunchroom in the basement of the West Meeting House for students from both campuses. While recruiting a new generation of memorable teachers and coaches like Wilbur E. "Toddy" Carr, Herman M. Magee, David S. Richie, and Robert M. Taylor, Reagan became known for his love of sports, his seventh-grade bird walks, his Scripture classes, and inspired Monday morning assemblies.

As enrollments from both Quaker and non-Quaker families grew, Reagan and the School Committee recognized the need for an expanded school on one campus. On the stretch of land that lay south of Main Street and behind the Academy building, the school soon embarked on a campaign that resulted in two new signature buildings: the one-story frame kindergarten building that opened in 1927, forever known as the White Building because of the paint color of its exterior; and the new high school,

The youngest MFS students take a break from recess to pose for the camera in 1929.

This architectural rendering showed the new junior-senior high school. Its construction represented a major milestone for Moorestown Friends School. Adorning the center of the three-story brick building was a cupola that would become a local landmark and symbol of the school for generations to come.

an expansive three-story brick building capped by a landmark cupola that faced south and echoed the gentle architectural lines of the nearby White Building. Designed for 300 students, the high school contained 13 classrooms, laboratories, an art room and workshops, a library, offices, and an unusual gymnasium/auditorium combination. In the fall of 1929, officials delayed the opening of school until September 30, when the new building was finished.

It was an exciting milestone. After nine years on two campuses, Moorestown Friends finally had one address. As the junior and senior high students explored their new building, the elementary school students moved back into classrooms in the Academy building. Eventually, the Meeting sold the former Friends' High School building at Second and Chester, and it was later demolished to make room for a new post office.

The MFS building campaign came with a hefty price tag—$275,000 for the two new buildings, 12 acres of land, and the purchase of a large house on Main Street known as Roberts Hall, which became a teachers' residence. After raising $47,000 to begin construction, the school was saddled with nearly $230,000 in debt, right when the Great Depression hit. Teachers and students give Reagan full credit for keeping the school open during these difficult times. He put a hold on all salaries and didn't once raise tuitions from 1930 to 1945, a step designed to keep cash-strapped families from leaving the school. To save money, he was also janitor and plumber; Reagan

MEMORY MILESTONE

We returned to the new Moorestown Friends High School in order to start our first and last year there. Not many lessons were done that day, as much time was spent in investigating the new building, discovering hidden rooms and hallways, and calculating the quickest method of getting from one end of the building to the other—some favored scooters, others velocipedes. It was all very new and unreal.

—September 30, 1929, seniors writing about opening day in the new high school

A 1933 kindergarten classroom provided the young students with plenty of room for art projects—and abundant light, thanks to the two walls of huge windows.

knew every fuse and plumbing connection in the new building, though he never mastered the electrical system that controlled the school bells. He knocked on doors to convince families—particularly Quaker families—to send their children to MFS. One summer, he and coach Herm Magee visited every rising senior to lobby for his or her return to school. Together with members of the School Committee, Reagan solicited donations to keep the school afloat.

Eventually, the scrimping paid off: in 1943, the school retired all debts associated with the new high school. In a special meeting, Reagan and members of the School Committee actually burned the mortgage, a scene applauded by members of prominent MFS Quaker families like Stokes and Matlack, Roberts and Sharpless, Cadbury and DeCou.

With the economic crisis barely behind him, Reagan then faced the challenges associated with World War II. In the winter of 1943–1944, MFS operated just one building as Reagan moved the elementary school students into every nook and cranny of the high school, a nod to shortages in money and heating resources. He convinced mothers to help out in the lunchroom, and pupils and faculty cleaned the classrooms. He started the school's first prekindergarten class and set up accelerated classes so senior boys about to become 18 and drafted could graduate at the end of the first term. The lack of gas and cars resulted

MEMORY MILESTONE

That was the kind of man Mr. Reagan was. He ran everything. He determined the admissions, was the business manager, ran faculty meetings, disciplined students, and handed out scholarships. He told us what to teach and how to teach it. It was teach, test, reteach, retest. The Depression years were not good years for independent schools, but under the indomitable leadership of Chester L. Reagan, Moorestown Friends School continued and grew.

—*Harrie B. Price III, hired by Reagan in 1952*

in fewer away games for the sports teams, but Reagan compensated with more intramural contests. He insisted school traditions like prom, the senior play, and the Red and Blue contests continue, and he and Mrs. Reagan still opened their home for the traditional fall faculty tea, the December Christmas party, and the graduation luncheon for seniors.

Though grandson T. Reagan Hull '62 once recalled that his grandfather was "somewhat of a stern, no-nonsense kind of guy," Reagan's penchant for quoting biblical passages or proverbs during Scripture classes and Monday morning assemblies actually seemed to soften him, reflecting a genuine strength of character and a devotion to Quaker education as he read from Psalm 46 ("Be still and know that I am God"), Proverbs 3:5–6 ("In all your ways acknowledge Him and He will make straight your paths"), and from Alexander Pope, the revered eighteenth-century English poet ("Tis education forms the common mind; Just as the twig is bent, the tree's inclined").

While Reagan steered the school through economic crisis, he also maintained the school's academic program. As the *Moorestown News* reported for the school's 150th Anniversary Supplement in May 1935: "High Scholastic Standard Upheld—Friends' Has Excellent Record in Preparing Students for College." The story listed every Ivy League school as well as Bryn Mawr, Vassar, Haverford, Swarthmore, Duke, Amherst, Williams, Trinity, and Earlham (Reagan's alma mater) as accepting MFS graduates. The students' success reflected the school's excellent teachers, and Reagan continued to recruit gifted faculty, including Harrie Price, Cully Miller, Neil Hartman, Herm Magee, and Floss Brudon.

By 1955, the year headmaster Merrill Hiatt arrived, this view from the Middle/Upper School steps showed the MFS athletic fields continuing to mature.

The old elementary school is pictured in 1964, before it was razed. The stone wall on the first floor of the building's western side was from the original stone schoolhouse built in 1785.

As Reagan entered his last decade at MFS, the public schools in Moorestown had become an attractive township asset and provided direct competition to the Quaker school. But by emphasizing MFS's ability to provide individual attention in a spiritual setting, Reagan continued to increase the school's enrollment until it reached 420 in 1955, Reagan's last year. In a dramatic shift from the days when only Quaker families attended Quaker schools, two-thirds of the students at MFS were now from non-Quaker families.

Overstating Chester Reagan's influence on Moorestown Friends would be difficult. Every school day for 30 years, Reagan walked from his home on Main Street, cut across the parking area behind the Meeting House, and made his way to his office. Instinctively, everyone understood it wasn't the path that was so important to Reagan, but the lasting shadows of integrity and conviction that he cast on his daily journey. While no one ever questioned Reagan's administrative skills, many would argue that his emphasis on student character, leadership, and Quaker ideals left permanent footprints.

When he retired, Reagan's final message to the Class of 1955 reflected both a lifetime of work and his challenge for their future: "Goodness, brotherly love, truth, and service," Reagan wrote, "think on these things."

Merrill L. Hiatt: 1955–1969

Merrill L. Hiatt arrived at MFS wearing brow-line glasses, a bowtie, and a white handkerchief in the breast pocket of his tweed suit. It was no coincidence that Hiatt, a former headmaster at Friends Academy in Locust Valley, Long Island, appeared dressed for business. For fourteen years at MFS, he brought a methodical, businesslike approach to the school, serving during a time of prosperity, a robust academic environment, and an increase in enrollment to over 600 students by 1969. "One of the most impressive characteristics of Moorestown Friends was that it was a stable

Archery was one of many sports offered by MFS as the school expanded its athletic repertoire almost as rapidly as its academic catalogue.

These Upper School students make use of the school's library in 1940. MFS has always been justifiably proud of its libraries, and later generations of students would come to enjoy one of the most sophisticated scholastic libraries in the region.

school with a stable faculty," said Hiatt, in one of his trademark, matter-of-fact summaries. "The School Committee was very cooperative, and we accomplished a great deal."

As birthrates climbed and the first wave of baby boomers reached school age, the challenges Hiatt faced were readily apparent. The jump in enrollment had squeezed every inch of available space out of the existing MFS facility. The school "failed to keep pace with the growth of its classes," the 1957 yearbook staff wrote, calling attention to the antiquated gymnasium and lack of laboratory space while dedicating their book to "the expansion movement."

In the fall of 1956, the School Committee approved a $250,000 building campaign that, by the end of 1957, resulted in an entire new wing constructed on the back of the high school building. The new wing contained six new classrooms and a biology laboratory. In 1959, a new gymnasium opened. The wooden tennis courts built during Reagan's tenure were demolished to make room for the new gymnasium.

As he worked to shore up the school's infrastructure, Hiatt focused on teacher salaries, which were below the median national average for comparable schools. He pushed to increase the median salary of the faculty to $5,000 by 1963, a 30 percent increase. The fact that substantial pay raises came at a time when Hiatt intentionally gave teachers more authority over the school didn't seem to bother anyone. "Chester was hands on, Merrill was hands off," said Neil Hartman, a revered mathematics and Scripture teacher who was hired in 1952. "We had a good relationship, and under Merrill the faculty took over the business meetings. We ran them. He was a good administrator, but not much of a people person."

By 1964, in a move that would forever trouble historical landmark purists, a study concluded that the elementary school had to go. Simply put, it would cost more to renovate than

Methodical and businesslike, Merrill Hiatt immediately began to tackle pressing issues at MFS when he was tapped as headmaster in 1955.

to tear down the delightfully quirky, ivy-covered building, a campus landmark that had already survived five additions and numerous renovations and yet still exhibited one wall from the original 1785 stone schoolhouse. To take its place, a simple but thoroughly modern, two-story Lower School with a brick façade took shape on the hillside rise above the White Building. This $350,000 construction campaign in 1965 also included renovations to the West Building to enlarge the kitchen/dining area, while turning the second-floor auditorium into a general-purpose room.

One thing that didn't change was the school's sense of Quaker values and its goal to educate the whole person—spirit, mind, and body. Though Hiatt

In 1965, construction commenced on a new elementary school. The previous building, though beloved and quirky, was deemed too expensive to renovate. The new $350,000 Lower School rose on a hill above the White Building.

The West Building was originally built as a Meeting House, but in later years was pressed into service as a gymnasium, with a portion of the dining hall located below the gym.

never approached the near-mythical Quaker status of Reagan, his quiet dedication to Quakerism resulted in expanded Scripture classes to include a broader religious education in the Upper School, the school's first international exchange programs, and the first Mock Political Conventions, inspired by social studies teacher George Macculloch "Cully" Miller to engage the entire school in the political process. In 1967, MFS's mission was rewritten as a cleaner, bolder statement of Quaker-based philosophy:

> *Moorestown Friends School seeks to combine the advantage of independent education with the values of the Quaker tradition . . . to encourage both independent thought and the pursuit of intellectual excellence . . . to achieve an environment characterized by candor, simplicity, adherence to conscience and service to others.*

In 1969, with a renovated campus, record enrollment, and a new Lower School completed, Hiatt retired. The prekindergarten classmates who entered MFS with him in 1955 were now seniors, and the yearbook editors noted the coincidence in their opening pages: "As we leave MFS . . . Mr. Hiatt too leaves, moving on, like us, to a new life, but remembered fondly and with much respect."

The new gym was built in 1959 during Merrill Hiatt's tenure, replacing the wooden tennis courts that had been constructed by his predecessor, Chester Reagan. The gym was just one of several facilities Hiatt's administration built.

Alexander M. MacColl: 1969–1986

On paper, Moorestown Friends School looked remarkably solid when Alexander M. MacColl took over from Hiatt in 1969. Enrollment was at an all-time high of 616, the school was fiscally sound, and buildings were in fine shape. MacColl specifically noted that he found the school "alive and well" when this father of six daughters was hired, a position that would tap into his previous experience as assistant headmaster at Friends Select and most recently as executive director of the Friends Neighborhood Guild, both in Philadelphia.

But in just one year, MFS did not look the same on anyone's piece of paper, particularly if that paper happened to be part of the annual MFS school yearbook. In a dramatic departure from the traditional yearbooks of the past, the 1970 *Cupola* reflected the times, featuring a purple cover with orange lettering, flashing psychedelic stars and fireworks symbols, and letting everyone know the "new" and "improved" *Cupola* had a not-so-subtle subtext: "Revolution." Inside, traditional formal head shots of senior males in coats and ties and senior females in sweaters and pearl necklaces gave way to highly individualistic photos and text.

As the yearbook made clear, it was a time of great social and political upheaval, triggered in part by lingering unrest associated with the assassinations of the Kennedy brothers and Martin Luther King Jr., the Vietnam War, the women's liberation movement, and the sexual revolution. Independent schools—often laboratories for questioning authority, independent thinking, and intellectual discourse—were, many times, the crucible for political, cultural, and philosophical controversies. MFS was no exception.

To many, MacColl was the right person for the job in these turbulent times. He came to MFS with a reputation as an innovative administrator, and true to form, he wasted little time in

When headmaster Alexander MacColl arrived at Moorestown Friends School in 1969, he inherited a school in great shape. But his term was on the cusp of great social upheaval in America and on his campus. Most considered him innovative, visionary, and inspirational, and felt he was the right man for the right time to handle this turmoil.

making changes. The fixed rows of desks gave way to informal classrooms and learning experiences as MacColl restructured the school's traditional academic program to provide out-of-classroom opportunities called Intensive Learning, Senior Projects, and hands-on, off-campus educational trips to places like Mystic Seaport—all designed to give richer context to classroom learning and textbook assignments. He encouraged

A little snow doesn't stop these young students, shown exiting the White Building for their next class.

faculty leadership at all levels of school management and sought student input on everything from curriculum changes to guidelines for student conduct. Committed to ethnic, racial, and economic diversity in a setting in which it was historically lacking, MacColl was instrumental in creating one of the most ambitious scholarship programs in the country, granting full awards to high school students from Camden through the MFS-Camden Community Scholarship Program.

Decades after his tenure at MFS, history would judge MacColl a visionary, a source of inspiration, and a leader who initiated the social programs and academic connections that would ultimately help define MFS.

But the dual whammy of social change from both within and outside the school proved to be challenging. From 1969 to 1975, enrollment at MFS plummeted from 616 to 443 students. Many parents simply could not deal with so much change in such a short time. Others feared their children were caught up in an educational experiment and wanted nothing to do with it.

"The enrollment decline came about in part over a fracture within the parent community," said Louis R. Matlack '53, the third generation of Matlacks to serve on the School Committee and the parent of three students during the MacColl years. "It had to do with, 'Let's stay the old

Watergate Special Prosecutor Archibald Cox visited MFS for the 1976 Mock Political Convention. To the left of Cox on the stage is Brad Bryen '78.

way' versus moving the school in new directions. The toughest time for the school was at the bottom of that enrollment dip, when you didn't know if it was going up the next year."

There was no magical moment when the struggling institution began to turn around, when parents decided to embrace MacColl's vision. What's clear, though, is that MacColl never stopped working to make both happen. Philip Lippincott, the former CEO of Scott Paper Co., and his wife Naomi, who had three children at the school during MacColl's tenure, worked to develop a crucial long-range strategic plan for the school. Enrollments began to inch back up. The size of the art and music program doubled, buoyed by the start of an annual Spring Parents Auction in 1976 that fully supported the first MFS Artist-in-Residence by 1983. The first graduates in the MFS-Camden scholarship program began to matriculate to some of the country's most competitive colleges, and each fall MacColl all but glowed as he welcomed new

Alex MacColl (standing sixth from right) and other students, faculty, and staff excavated under the Auditorium in 1970.

Classmates Janet Stevens '77 (left) and Joan Rosenberg '77 take a break from their work. Stevens credited Alex MacColl for instilling in her a passion to study global issues. It was "life changing," she would say in later years. "He just pushed you . . . and he knew you could take it."

ninth graders from Camden into the school. Teacher salaries increased, along with cooperation among the faculty, School Committee, parents, and students, to determine the goals and objectives of the school. Said longtime teacher Cully Miller, "We became a more democratic institution." MacColl pushed for more successful annual giving and capital campaigns, and grew a meager $97,000 endowment to over $2 million by 1986.

In an era marked by dramatic change, not everything was completely new. Linking the past to the present, MacColl, the School Committee, and Moorestown Friends Meeting created the Chester Reagan Chair in Faith and Practice to integrate Quaker studies throughout the school and to enhance the school's commitment to community service. And the echoes of old-fashioned school spirit returned to campus when the boys varsity soccer team won the state championship in double overtime in 1979, followed in June 1980 when a lacrosse team led by coaching legend Floss Brudon won

the state championship by defeating Moorestown High School. With two daughters on the team, MacColl wore both parent and headmaster hats while cheering from the sidelines.

MacColl never doubted that MFS was on the right path. "I believed in the strength of the school," he said. And with time, the extended school community and students like Janet N. Stevens '77 believed in it, too.

After leaving a public school to join MFS in the seventh grade, Stevens began to participate in what she called "life-changing experiences" through Intensive Learning projects on Philadelphia and city issues, welfare rights and children, and the Palestinian-Israeli conflict in the Middle East. Though many of her classmates disliked the school's new learning environment, Stevens soon grasped the value in reading controversial books that parents didn't want students to read, understanding for the first time that child abuse existed while she "lived such a blessed life," and realizing that there were many sides to every story in international conflict. "And it was all because of Alex MacColl. He was one of my favorite teachers of all time, a great classroom teacher who brought the world and issues to you and then took you out of that room to see them firsthand," remembers Stevens. "He was dynamic, and he just pushed you. He made you think on your toes, and he pushed you to a level of being uncomfortable, and he knew you could take it."

In the fall of 1985, as MFS began its Bicentennial Celebration, MacColl stood on the speaker's platform and looked out over a sunshine-filled courtyard, packed with people sitting on the lawn and standing under the trees. The scene was absolutely beautiful. As a welcoming gesture, students suspended class flags from each window of the Upper School, and flags bearing the red and blue MFS seal

Involved, hands on, and approachable, Alexander MacColl left MFS in 1986. "We are challenged to provide our students with a lifelong love of learning," he told a gathering a year earlier. It was part challenge, part dare, and 100 percent MacColl.

Doing Well and Doing Good 39

Students are always eager to head to the playground for recess.

lined the pathways. The Senior High Choir sang the school song, the MFS Ensemble played, and at one point MacColl turned to then-governor Thomas Kean to unveil the MFS Bicentennial banner, which would soon stretch across Main Street for all to see.

"We are challenged to provide young people with a lifelong love of learning and commitment to a just and equitable society," MacColl said. "It is a goal that shapes our programs and attitudes today and continues as a priority as we enter our third century."

It was a defining moment for MacColl. Both he and the school had survived nearly 17 years of dramatic change, a period of time that, in the context of a 200-year history, might not seem all that important. But on a day when the past and present collided, it finally seemed to dawn on those present that Alexander MacColl had done something extraordinary when he first challenged the status quo in 1969: MacColl helped define the future for Moorestown Friends School by daring to envision how great it could be.

Gardiner Bridge: 1986–1987; Clinton P. Wilkins: 1987–1990

Six months after the school's Bicentennial Celebration, MacColl announced his resignation. "I believe that as our school embarks on its third century, new leadership will best enable MFS to respond creatively to the challenges . . . in the years ahead," wrote MacColl on April 15, 1986.

The timing took many by surprise. After all, enrollment, that barometer of school success, had returned in 1986 to around 600 students, nearly identical to the count when MacColl first arrived in 1969. The school had just broken ground for its first construction project in 20 years, and everyone agreed MacColl was instrumental in raising $1 million for Stokes Hall, a new building designed to link Upper and Lower Schools and create one centralized library.

But MacColl and members of the School Committee had agreed that it was time for new

Gardiner Bridge came from Texas in 1986 to serve as Moorestown Friends School's interim headmaster upon Alex MacColl's resignation.

Clinton Wilkins oversaw the opening of Stokes Hall.

leadership. School Committee members knew maintaining enrollment would be a challenge and more efforts to attract students that fit the school's academically rigorous mission were essential. In January 1986, MacColl hired the school's first director of admissions. And while no one doubted MacColl's close relationship with the faculty, the School Committee concluded there were limits to what a school run by a democracy of teachers could accomplish. Too many teachers, it seemed, now taught courses that reflected personal interests instead of curriculum-based standards. Important academic connections between Lower, Middle, and Upper Schools were noticeably missing.

Instead of rushing to find MacColl's replacement, the School Committee hired Gardiner Bridge from Texas to serve as its interim head of school from mid-1986 to mid-1987. But the news about Bridge, a fatherly figure with considerable experience in independent schools and interim management, did not go over well.

Enrollment dropped to 572 during Bridge's one year at MFS, and then dipped further to 533 students in 1987. The School Committee soon announced it had hired a new head of school: Clint Wilkins, the assistant headmaster and former principal of the Upper School at Sidwell Friends, would take over MFS in the summer of 1987.

For Wilkins, MFS represented his first opportunity to run a school. "I was looking for a major challenge, exactly what Moorestown offered me," recalled Wilkins, who was married and the father of three young children. At MFS, Wilkins supervised the opening of Stokes Hall, and worked with the School Committee to write an overarching statement of purpose. But he simply could not get ahead of the school's problems. "I gave it a good try," he remembered. "But the bottom line is that I was a transitional figure in the life cycle of the school. It was a tough period for the school, and for me and my family. It was not a good fit."

The School Committee agreed. By the time Wilkins left in 1990, enrollment dropped to 485, and the decreased tuition revenue had begun to impact the school's bottom line. With a reported deficit in the six figures, the school cut back on all

discretionary spending, postponed some building maintenance, and dipped into a line of credit to help pay the bills. "There was a relatively small group that appreciated how difficult the financial situation was," said Thomas E. Zemaitis, an MFS parent who joined the School Committee in 1991 and learned about the problems in retrospect. "I knew about the crisis of leadership, but I did not realize the depth of the school's financial problems. It was an eye-opening experience."

In 1990, MFS began the search for its fourth head of school in six years.

Alan R. Craig: 1990–2001

In the winter of 1990, a seasoned educator named Alan R. Craig visited MFS. This lifelong teacher and administrator, who had served for the past 18 years in various leadership positions at Friends Academy in Locust Valley, New York, immediately looked past the school's enrollment crisis, its budget problems, and the walls that needed paint. Instead, he focused on the teachers who needed leadership, the good programs that required direction, and a school crying out for someone ready to take on its challenges. "I liked everything I saw," said Craig, who possessed that quintessentially charming, outsized personality that seemed to shout "Where do we start?" whenever he walked into a room. "I loved the fact that it would be a lot of work. I loved the challenges."

A sigh of relief came over the MFS community when Fred T. Moriuchi, School Committee clerk, announced that a man with a great sense of humor and "wise in the ways

Alan R. Craig landed at MFS in 1990 and found budget issues, an enrollment crisis, and buildings in need of repair. "I liked everything I saw," he later recalled. "I loved the fact that it would be a lot of work." The MFS community breathed a sigh of relief, while Craig's fondness for hard work began paying dividends. By the time he left in 2001, the school was once again a shining star on Main Street.

Often leaving his office for his so-called "kid fix," Alan Craig was beloved by the students, even if he did make them spit out their gum. He addressed faculty turnover and admissions, not only raising enrollment but doing so with higher standards.

of schools" would join MFS on July 1, 1990. Any remnant of a leadership crisis flew out the door the minute Alan Craig walked into his Stokes Hall office. Craig was the boss. He exuded confidence.

"He was the best pedagogue I have ever met as an administrator," said Matlack, who teamed with Jack McKeon to lead the search committee. "He could come into a classroom and tell you what the teacher was trying to do, what they needed to do, and what they could change in order to do their job. He was a natural at it; it was a gift, and he was a wonderful mentor."

Craig had barely unpacked before he decided to spruce up the place. He ripped up old carpets and convinced parents to adopt different floors and pay for new floor tiles. He picked out blue and white paint for the walls, creating an "MFS blue" to visually unite the school hallways. He asked that venetian blinds in classrooms be drawn halfway before teachers left for the day, to give the school a more uniform exterior look. He hired Larry Brandimarto to be the new physical facilities manager, ensuring that the grounds and buildings were always in top shape. He put up a new sign that gave Moorestown Friends School more of a presence on Main Street, a symbolic shout out that was lost on no one.

Without hesitating, Craig took ownership of running the school. Explained Craig, "I knew that the board had been micromanaging. So I said, 'Who runs the school—the board or the head?' and they said, 'We're tired of running the school,' and that was that." He introduced zero-based budgeting and looked for every imaginable way to cut costs—from making faculty and staff pay for their yearbooks to asking his wife, Mary, to cater receptions and fund-raising events, which the Craigs called "friendraising." There was a fair amount of administrative and faculty turnover, and Craig created considerable controversy when, one-by-one, he replaced the Lower, Middle, and Upper School directors with his own team. He immediately balked at the concept of faculty meetings run by faculty, where concerns had to be written down on paper and vetted. "So I said to the faculty, 'Every second week is your meeting, every other week is mine. Mine are compulsory, and *I'm* running the meeting.'"

When it came to admissions, Craig worked to improve the academic profile of incoming students. "We had to decide what kind of school we were *going* to be, and we had to admit who we *wanted* to be," he said. For a while, Craig personally reviewed every admissions decision. "We set our standards, and then we set them higher. The word went out, and our enrollment started to climb." By 1992, enrollment was up to 506, and it never dipped below 500 again, steadily rising to 652 during Craig's tenure.

Craig certainly had his share of critics. But the faculty and others learned to appreciate the strengths of a leader who didn't necessarily try to reinvent the school but worked to make the core elements of the school stronger. And every time Craig invited students into his office to talk about their school experiences or wandered the halls in search of what he called a "kid fix," it was evident that the critics who mattered most adored this head of school—even if he did make them spit out their gum. "It was so much fun to watch Alan work with the kids," said William Guthe, a Moriuchi family in-law, parent of three MFS students, and a member of the search committee that interviewed Craig in 1990. "He had a nice touch with all the

The Dining Hall Commons was built in 1997 during Alan Craig's administration. It was one of several capital improvements to the campus he implemented.

kids, but one neat thing about Alan is that he really understood what life was like for the Camden kids. He used to stay late, and he would give them a ride home. The pride and the ownership he took in the school were wonderful."

Though he wasn't a Quaker, Craig was respectful of Quaker values and careful to nurture relationships with School Committee members, especially key members he called the "weighty Quakers," those who supported the school "morally and financially, and accepted my style—which was pretty hard-core," Craig admitted. Looking to strengthen the Quaker-based programs throughout MFS, Craig expanded the Chester Reagan Chair established by his predecessor to include not only a coordinator for Upper School but an additional coordinator for Lower and Middle School. "The Quaker Ladies," as the Quaker educators were soon known, were more intentional about making Quaker values an even more integral part of every aspect of student life.

Craig stayed at MFS for 11 years. When asked to review the progress made at the school during his tenure, Craig doesn't rush to mention Campaign 2000, which raised over $2 million and allowed MFS to create two computer labs, establish the Endowment for Faculty Support, contribute $500,000 to the Annual Sustaining Fund, and build the Dining Hall Commons in 1997. He doesn't initially talk about renovating the West Building in 1999, and he doesn't brag about the Campaign for Arts, Athletics and Endowment—an effort that began in the fall of 1998 and resulted in the largest single contribution and challenge match in the history of the school that would build the new Field House and renovate the Arts Center.

Mark Baiada, Alan Craig, and Cindy Eni Yingling '75 enter the Dining Hall Commons at the 1998 ribbon-cutting ceremony. The trio spearheaded the Campaign 2000 effort.

Instead, Craig talks about the atmosphere of MFS, of dancing at May Day, shaking hands at graduation, hosting staff parties at his home, or sitting on the classroom floor surrounded by students at the annual Thanksgiving Happening. "I just loved the atmosphere."

The biggest gift that Alan Craig brought to Moorestown Friends School in his 11 years as head of school isn't found in a new building façade or captured in a capital

The Dining Hall Commons is a great place for friends to touch base.

campaign. Rather, it's that "ah-ha" moment when you honestly look past an institution's imperfections and recognize how truly remarkable it is; when you believe so much in a school like MFS that the tireless work to make it better is downright joyful; when, after a long day at school, you open the front door that looks out over the Oval and you stand there, scanning the buildings and the athletic fields teeming with student-athletes and coaches, and you completely understand why people say they love this school.

Laurence R. Van Meter: 2001–

When Laurence R. Van Meter returned to Moorestown Friends School on July 1, 2001, he was the first head of school who played with blocks in the White Building when he was four years old. Which means that Larry Van Meter is an original—an MFS graduate who never went to school anywhere else from prekindergarten to 12th grade. His MFS legacy includes rolling sticky dates for the Friendship Fair in the third grade, the humiliation of being a sixth-grade boy in tights on May Day, competing every year on Color Day (Blue!),

Larry Van Meter was determined to take a fresh look at the school he was being charged to helm. Tapping his extensive business and management skills, he shepherded into place a strategic plan in 2004 that would turn "a very good school into a great school."

and knowing where to find the key that opened the door that led to the forbidden Cupola when he was a senior. He certainly remembers the day that a handful of carefully hidden, wind-up alarm clocks went off during Meeting for Worship (he prefers not to discuss that).

But make no mistake: When Van Meter returned to Moorestown Friends to become its eighth head of school, he was not interested in reliving the past. Instead, this deeply introspective Quaker educator, who brought over 30 years of diverse educational and professional experiences to his new job, has always been intent on moving beyond the school's history by staying focused on the future.

Probably few heads of school in the country went in more directions in their life before returning to the same school they attended as a child than Larry Van Meter '68. A Moorestown native, Van Meter enjoyed careers in conservation, marketing, teaching, and running a nonprofit, while finding time somewhere along the way to earn an MBA. When he arrived at MFS in 2001, he brought with him not only his wife, Margaret, and two children, Luke and Matty, but a lifetime of experiences that came to bear on the place where it all started for him.

From the moment Van Meter filled out his application statement for the head of school position, he has been remarkably clear about his institutional goals for MFS: he wants to run a school where Quaker values are explicit in every level of the school.

"At a Friends School, the Quaker ethos should suffuse the educational experience," he wrote. "This means being knowledgeable, not just in an area of narrow, technical competence, but in broader areas of culture and science. It means being thoughtful, tolerant, open-minded, and compassionate. It means being aware of the importance of living a principled life, of recognizing the positive and negative influences of popular culture, of understanding the difference between things of transitory value and those that are lasting. It means self-interest tempered by a deep and abiding concern for others and for preserving the earth—for living sustainably and understanding the interconnectedness of all beings and all actions."

Van Meter looked to lead MFS forward by tapping into his background of diverse professional experiences that in many ways distinguished him from his predecessors, and was in many ways a reflection of the broad and innovative curriculum he had experienced himself at Moorestown Friends. With the exception of Alex MacColl, every MFS administrator before Van Meter had worked exclusively within the educational system, and Van Meter's resume revealed a decidedly less traditional career path that included the following: executive director of a small but influential Vermont conservation organization; a second degree (his first was in history from Hamilton College) from Rochester Institute of Technology in Woodworking and Furniture Design, followed by teaching at The Mountain School in Vermont; executive director of the Appalachian Trail Conference, a national nonprofit with 20,000 members; graduating with honors with an MBA degree from the Tuck School at Dartmouth; director of marketing for Thos. Moser Cabinetmakers—and, at last, a return to the educational arena as director of advancement at George School in Newtown, Pennsylvania; headmaster of the Darrow School, a coeducational boarding school in New York; and then head of school at Moorestown Friends.

These fourth graders are enjoying "Hoagies with the Head," in which they are welcomed into the Van Meter household to have sandwiches and discuss life at Moorestown Friends School. These feedback sessions, which Van Meter also conducts with eighth grade and Upper School students, are as important to him in their own way as are discussions with the School Committee.

At MFS, Van Meter pulled successfully from every facet of his unique professional path to bring new perspectives and strengths to the school. This educator with considerable business and management experience—who had earned a reputation for turning around organizations with unclear goals, considerable financial woes, and ill-defined strengths—could formulate a strategic plan, write an incisive critique of a classroom, project the marginal cost of another student in fifth grade, and talk knowledgeably about spreadsheets.

Head of School Larry Van Meter with third graders at Camp Bernie in 2009.

And though Van Meter definitely looked to the touchstones that sustained the strongest leaders before him—the deep Quaker convictions of Chester Reagan, the diversity initiatives and experiential learning programs of Alex MacColl, and the strong community relationships built by Alan Craig—he nonetheless relied primarily on the depth of his educational and professional background to take a fresh look at MFS and decide what was missing. The result? A strategic plan in 2004 that Van Meter believes will transform "a very good school into a great school."

The 2004 strategic plan is a blueprint for the future of Moorestown Friends School. While many such documents get tossed on the shelf a few months after they are written, everyone at MFS refers to the plan as a living document, one that guides school decisions in 2010 as much as it did when it was first proposed. In the last five years, it has resulted in increased Advanced Placement courses, additional language and science options, and a high school Honors Program designed to further enhance the school's commitment to academic rigor. Also, it has allowed for the physical expansion of the campus through the acquisition of surrounding properties like the Acme building and the Greenleaf. These purchases will soon ease existing classroom shortages and create a campus for both today's needs and into the future. In addition, the plan resulted in salary increases for teachers, a renewed focus on increasing the diversity of both staff and students, and the development of the school's "Examined Life" program, where students make important connections between what they learn in the classroom and how they perceive their roles in their larger communities.

Moorestown Friends School has enjoyed certain hands-on skills from all of its heads of school, whether it was repairing the boiler or simply helping to paint walls. But Larry Van Meter's degree in woodworking and furniture design from the Rochester Institute of Technology was especially handy in helping students construct the replica of a 200-year-old Hollinshead clock that now chimes from the Stokes Hall lobby. Here he works with Doug Boyer '09 and Chris Lojek '09.

"When I say a 'great' school, I am talking about a school that combines the twin pillars of academic rigor with spiritual and ethical awareness," said Van Meter. "We will not sacrifice one for the other. The combination of the two is what we should be about— graduates who are gifted academically, who think critically, who are in touch with their spiritual side, and want to do well in the world."

As Van Meter incorporates this vision into the everyday life of some 700 students, he clearly wrestles with

decisions impacting the lives of students and teachers. He is a unique combination of leader and mentor, someone who understands the inherent challenges in creating a school environment where students are valued as individuals but encouraged to come together as a community, which speaks to the very heart of a Quaker education.

As Van Meter leads MFS forward, he taps into a strength that simply did not exist for his predecessors: Van Meter has the gift of institutional experience. When he worries about the possibility of declining enrollment in tough economic times, he recalls that Chester Reagan came to his house, and asked his parents to send him and his two siblings to Moorestown Friends. When he's hit with criticism about the recent purchase of nearby buildings and properties, he understands that his predecessors, in good times and bad, "took the long view in ensuring that our students received a top-notch academic and spiritual education." When students struggle in class and Van Meter meets with them to talk about problem solving and resilience, he remembers what it was like to be an average fifth grader, looking out the window at the construction of the new gym instead of paying attention to Mrs. Allis Borton's arithmetic lessons. When he meets with alumni, he relishes their stories about teaching icons named Cully Miller, Sandy Heath, Neil Hartman, Jean Ricketts, Harrie Price, Herm Magee, Davie Weiner, and Floss Brudon, knowing the stories of future alumni will one day resonate with the names of today's excellent teachers. He marvels at the diversity of today's student body, noting it is both the single biggest change in the school since he was a student and one of the most important differences for students today.

And when life and school collide, when the school community faces deep personal loss or world events take a tragic turn, Van Meter knows to guide them to the restorative quiet, the promise of healing that comes from the Meeting House.

Laurence R. Van Meter '68, who grew up in Moorestown and sometimes walked to school, will forever be the first graduate to come back and run Moorestown Friends School. "It makes a difference," said Lynne D. Brick, the mother of three MFS graduates and the Lower and Middle School Quaker education coordinator, "when your head is a Quaker and can point back to the White Building."

CHAPTER 3

QUAKER TRADITIONS

AND COMMITMENT TO DIVERSITY

Moorestown Friends School is a community dedicated to the pursuit of educational excellence for a diverse student body within an academically rigorous and balanced program emphasizing personal, ethical, and spiritual growth.

—Moorestown Friends School Mission Statement 1987, revised 2004

CELEBRATING 225 YEARS
OF QUAKER EDUCATION

The mission statement is the first thing you see when you enter Stokes Hall at Moorestown Friends School: the printed words form a colorful, burgundy border near the ceiling in the lobby. The message underscores the Quaker values that guide the school, a constant and defining factor in the school's educational experience since it was founded 225 years ago. And it is the key to understanding what noted Quaker author Robert Smith '41, former headmaster at Sidwell Friends School, meant when he wrote, "Friends schools are unabashedly in the business of making better people."

Lower School Spanish teacher Erick Perez works with a student in class.

Quaker Values

As students and faculty walk each day beneath the words of the mission statement, they proceed to classes and activities that reflect the emphasis on Quaker values in ways that undergird the school's philosophy and, therefore, its attitude toward education and young people. Consider:

I Care

In the prekindergarten class taught by Lisa Thomas Martin '84, four-year-olds look to the "I Care Cat," a treasured MFS tradition that uses a cat puppet to introduce concepts of caring in actions and thoughts. Some "I Care" rules? "We listen to each other." "Hands are for helping, not hurting." "We use 'I Care' language like thank you, please, I'm sorry." "We are responsible for what we say and do."

The "Quaker Ladies"

The "Quaker Ladies"—Priscilla Taylor-Williams, Chester Reagan Chair of Religious and Quaker Studies, and Lynne Brick, Lower School/Middle School Quaker education coordinator—guide new students through Quaker orientation, reinforcing the Quaker messages of community, equality, peace, integrity, and compassion. "Being Quaker," Taylor-Williams often tells a student body represented by many different religious affiliations, "is a way to live."

Meeting for Worship

Once a week, students as young as kindergarten gather in the Meeting House for Meeting for Worship. The fourth, eighth, and twelfth graders sit on the raised, facing

MEMORY MILESTONE

As I reflect on a significant number of years as a teacher, an administrator, a parent, and presently a trustee, I recognize a unifying theme as delineated in the MFS mission statement with the key words "personal, ethical, and spiritual growth." Quakerism has always been taught at MFS, but for me after three decades, this resonates more clearly today. The relevance to Quaker thinking as reflected in the mission statement has gradually become a vibrant concept. . . . This awareness of "personal, ethical, and spiritual growth" is reflected in the interactions among the students, faculty, administration, and staff, and guides trustees in their deliberations. Thus, this has become a core element of the school community. Like Quakerism, it is not taught as one teaches mathematics but is gradually absorbed. This is growth worth celebrating.

—Grace Kennedy Blackburn, School Committee member

benches, a position that puts them "in care" of the Meeting as they look out over the rows of students in their respective division. They sit in silence, listening carefully to those who are moved to speak and thinking about their connection to God. Sitting in silence is often difficult, they are reminded, but there is an unspoken power in sitting together as one.

"Mix It Up at Lunch"

In the Dining Hall Commons, director of multicultural affairs Karen Washington guides students through a "Mix It Up at Lunch" day to promote awareness that social boundaries can lead to divisions and exclusion—all by sitting at lunch with someone a student didn't know.

Community Service

A note posted on the Upper School bulletin board asks, "Looking for a way to do your service hours?" The suggestions are endless—helping in the Extended Day/ Afterschool programs, collecting scarves, boxing holiday meals, teaching robotics

Students eat in shifts in the Dining Hall Commons throughout the late morning and early afternoon. Bright and airy with wooden trusses, the Commons is a favorite spot for students and faculty alike to catch up on news of the day.

at a school in Camden. As a condition of graduation, each senior is required to perform 50 hours of service—a reflection of the Quaker tradition to "let your life speak."

Since it was founded in the 17th century, the Society of Friends, or Quakers, has always believed that spiritual, social, and intellectual growth are closely linked, and stressed that a child's education should develop all three. Consistent with the fundamental Quaker belief that there is that of God in every person and that every person is important, a Quaker education strives to focus on the needs of each individual student.

And while encouraging each individual to think independently, a Quaker education also reinforces the importance of working together as a community and being responsible for the community around you. This testimony has driven Quaker schools to emphasize service and service learning, long before it was a mainstream, politically correct concept.

"No pains will be spared to arouse and stimulate the best in each individual pupil," stated the Friends' High School 1891–1892 catalog. "The teachers will continually strive to

MEMORY MILESTONE

I think we all feel we got a great academic education. We learned to think on our feet and be very analytical, to work in a team environment while respecting the individual and respecting the Quaker values that are integrated as part of the whole. Because MFS blends and creates such strong linkages across these experiences, I think it creates, if you will, very admirable thought leaders who are really good human beings. That is really, for me, a true differentiating factor. There are a lot of places you can go to get a great education, but not a lot of places you can go to that create good human beings, who have this mind-set that they want to help. That is part of what is built into the curriculum.

—Ken Zekavat '80, parent and School Committee member

develop that love for knowledge, interest in the welfare of humanity and careful, thoughtful mode of acting so desirous in young people." According to the Friends' Academy 1899 catalog: "The School aims to give each pupil such careful individual attention in his work and in his play that will bring out the best in him. . . ."

When Quaker students, families, and faculty made up most, if not all, of the student body, the school's embrace of Quaker values was all but unspoken; in 1920, Moorestown Friends School needed only to offer midweek Meeting for Worship and Scripture classes to reinforce its Quaker roots. Gradually, as fewer Quakers came to the school and fewer Quaker families lived in Moorestown and the surrounding communities, the school leaders added new programs. In the 1950s, for instance, the students formed a Religious Life Committee to ensure that the student body received "a spiritual as well as academic education," resulting in Tuesday morning assemblies, class discussions, and queries in Meeting.

Third-grade teacher Ted Quinn discusses Russia with his young students. From early on, MFS students learn that the world extends far beyond Moorestown.

From kindergarten through graduation, students at Moorestown Friends School interact with any one of more than 400 campus computers on a daily basis, including these in the library. Computers are used for everything from teaching geometry to music theory. Classes, including major and minor offerings, range from AP Computer Science to Media Arts to Technology in Business to Fashion and Photoshop.

Over time, the percentage of Quaker students at MFS dropped to less than 5 percent, reflecting a similar pattern of decline in the local Quaker population among Moorestown's 20,000 residents. In a township once dominated by Quaker families, by 1980 less than 2 percent of the township's residents were Friends. With fewer Quaker families and students, the school's efforts to integrate Quaker values became more deliberate and visible. Meeting for Worship has stayed exactly the same, but Scripture classes were recast as religious studies, which have now evolved into an entire curriculum of religion and philosophy that today includes 12 courses spanning art, history, and global politics. In 1977, Head of School Alex MacColl, Tom DeCou '30, and School Committee members Louis Matlack, Tak Moriuchi, and Lydia Stokes launched an endowment to establish the Chester Reagan Chair, a faculty position devoted to religion and ethics programs in the Upper School, in memory of the former Quaker headmaster. Many members of the school community joined in making gifts to build the endowment.

Today, Quaker values are integrated into classroom programs and curricula at every grade level. Two full-time religious education teachers focus on spiritual and ethical issues and community involvement. Two service coordinators promote and monitor the school's service learning program. The former Upper School Student Government has transitioned to a Meeting for Worship for Business format in the Friends tradition.

MEMORY MILESTONE

On many levels, Moorestown Friends School to me is really a school of true "friends." I am sure other people experienced this sense of warmth, caring, and belonging at MFS, but I believe this is what has made MFS such a special place to so many people.

—Beth Clauss Freeland '81

A Commitment to Diversity

MFS's strong commitment to diversity of many kinds is evident throughout the school, with Karen Washington, director of multicultural affairs, overseeing cultural diversity initiatives. Lower School has a thematic multicultural curriculum with activities and lessons ranging from third-grade study of Native American history and culture to the kindergarten's annual "trip" to Hawaii. Through Quaker education classes and the celebration of holidays belonging to many different religious and cultural traditions, students are exposed to ways of living different from their own and are taught to honor those differences. In Middle School, students are engaged in deeper conversations about respect for the individual. Middle School is a place where self begins to come into focus. Upper School students are afforded extensive opportunities to grow in the area of diversity awareness. Topics are woven into the curriculum, including elective offerings such as "Equity and Social Justice," "Diversity in the Media," "Women's Studies," "Gender Studies," and "Race, Gender

MEMORY MILESTONE

I believe that the Camden Scholars Program may have saved my life. The personal attention I received from my teachers and staff there helped me to better understand my personal learning style and was very helpful in my development as a student and a person. It was an excellent opportunity to gain the education that I knew in my heart I deserved, but otherwise would not have been able to afford.

—*Tiffany Taylor Jenkins '97*

and Identity in Literature." Students may choose from a myriad of clubs (such as the Gay-Straight Alliance; the Gender Equality Forum, providing a place to discuss issues of particular importance to women; and the Jewish Culture Club).

Faculty and staff maintain a Diversity Committee, and SEED (Seeking Educational Equity and Diversity) seminars are offered throughout the year.

The long-standing Camden Scholars Program, offering nearly full-tuition scholarships, has included more than 100 participants and more than 90 alumni. Camden Scholars started with ninth-grade students from Camden in the 1970s when MFS partnered with A Better Chance (ABC), a national nonprofit designed to increase the number of promising minority students in independent schools. In 1983, MFS took over the program, providing funding through the school's financial aid budget and valued scholarship donors.

The range of programs, clubs, subjects, and activities at MFS is extensive enough that it's almost impossible for a student not to have something to keep his or her attention.

Beginning in 2000, the program expanded to include seventh graders, and science teacher Tina Wheaton Corsey is the program's coordinator. "The networks of support within the program have really nourished a lot of students in a lot of ways," said former MFS Upper School director Mary Williams. "It is a true testimony to Friends' principles."

In addition to Quakers and a variety of other Protestant denominations, a wide range of religious faiths are represented by students, such as Roman Catholicism, Judaism, Hinduism, Sikhism, Islam, and others. The school's rising financial aid budget, which is now 15 percent of the operating budget, also helps provide socioeconomic diversity.

MEMORY MILESTONE

Wednesdays were the hardest. Forty minutes of silence and sitting. For me at that young age, it seemed like someone was out to get me. . . . I can remember trying to count as high as I could for 40 minutes. I don't think I ever made it past a few hundred. I can remember trying to stare at one spot on the wall for the duration of Meeting. No dice. I can remember trying to conjugate verbs in Spanish or reviewing the sine of 30° and other trigonometry problems. All of these things helped to pass the time, but I seemed, then, to be missing the point. Meeting for Worship was not a chore or a challenge, but a gift. Each week, we put down our cell phones; we turn off our iPods; we stop writing, and calculating, and producing, and we sit. And think. And reflect.

—*Steven Porter '98*

Tying It All Together

"One of the criticisms that Friends schools always get from their Meeting is that they aren't 'Quaker' enough," said parent Kiyo Moriuchi '71. "If anyone says that about MFS, they haven't been here lately."

In 2004, the School Committee further reinforced its Quaker culture by adding the words "community" and "ethical" to its mission statement, the one now painted boldly near the school entrance. This revision resulted in the centerpiece of the 2004 strategic plan, a program called "The Examined Life," a phrase drawn from Socrates' axiom, "The unexamined life is not worth living." Through its spiritual and ethical education,

MFS is committed to developing students who have learned how to live an examined life characterized by four important elements: critical thought, openness to the Spirit, ethical development, and resilience.

"I think of them as a Rubik's cube," said Taylor-Williams, who is referred to as "PTW" by students who frequently stop by her office, just off the Stokes Lobby. "You can pull them all apart, but they all intersect at one point. Our expression of 'tough minds, tender hearts' comes from the concept of putting ethics and critical thinking together. Openness to the Spirit is fundamentally Quaker. And we also recognized that doing well requires resilience, because the world will always throw you a curve and resilience is part of being a functioning adult."

Affirmation that a Quaker education works—that it provides the transformational experience MFS leaders like to talk about—is usually as close as the nearest MFS alum. "The way I see the world, and the way I interact with people, is a not-so-subtle reflection of what was instilled in me at MFS every day," said Mark Mitchell '86, a Camden Scholar and now vice president for school information services at the National Association of Independent Schools. "The whole idea of respecting that there is that of God in everyone is something that I think about literally every day."

For 30 years, the Camden Scholars Program has provided opportunities to students in the Camden School District.

4

A snapshot of teaching and learning at MFS today, inside and outside of the classroom.

THE EDUCATIONAL CORE:
A Look at an MFS Education

CELEBRATING 225 YEARS
OF QUAKER EDUCATION

In a marketing campaign called "Great Kids, Going Places," Moorestown Friends turns the spotlight on exceptional students and their accomplishments. But these mini-profiles of graduates serve another purpose, too. Each highlights the dynamic educational experience at MFS, where dedicated faculty members work in classrooms every day to present a rigorous academic curriculum in an atmosphere that embraces active learning, critical thinking, and individual growth.

Rebecca Salowe '09—an Academic All-American field hockey and lacrosse player, the producer of a *Science among Friends* podcast, now at the University of Pennsylvania—seemed to describe the MFS sixth-grade art history class when she said, "MFS classes revolve around discussion rather than lecture. Students feel free to share an opposing opinion or theory; individuality is not only respected, but expected." In Richard Marcucci's art history course, Middle School students are free to debate the often-confusing elements of modern art, question whether

Picasso was the father of cubism or modernism or both, and debate whether they even like an early work by Vincent van Gogh.

Kendra Whitfield '09—a National Achievement Scholarship Outstanding Participant and dancer attending Georgetown University—all but pictured a Jacqueline Zemaitis Lower School Winter Concert when she said, "The MFS community is filled with encouraging people who genuinely care about your success as a student and as an individual." As Lower School music teacher, Zemaitis believes that every voice is worth hearing, every child is worth celebrating, and every child who wants to sing a solo will sing a solo.

And Russell Hensley '09—a member of the championship robotics team, varsity cross-country team, and string ensemble before matriculating at Carnegie Mellon University—surely had the robotics program's outreach efforts in mind when he noted, "MFS is a close-knit community with motivated students and a motivated faculty." Under the guidance of Upper School physics teacher Tim Clarke, MFS students now work with elementary and middle school students in Camden and Philadelphia to broaden their understanding of physics and help them prepare for the exciting and challenging world of robotics competition.

Middle School English teacher Debra Muzyka Casne assists a student with an assignment. In Middle School, students develop critical thinking and decision-making skills, while tackling a wide array of literature and strengthening their writing and oral skills. They make connections among the written word, society, and their own lives.

Since it was founded in 1785, the educational core of MFS has emphasized Quaker values, small classes, individual attention, hands-on learning, and an academically rigorous program that prepares students for college. Since the late 1800s, it has also included arts and sports—in fact, the 1899 yearbook boasts of "facilities for *Drawing rarely equaled* by schools anywhere," while the 1920 catalogue notes that "a strong, vigorous body is absolutely essential to the best mental development." Early exchange programs with students in France and Germany helped expand the students' understanding of the world, while the growth of innovative community service projects and outreach programs closer to home helped broaden a student's perception of real-world challenges that often weren't so visible from the MFS Oval. "We tried to instill a desire to think in our students," Warren Shelley Jr., longtime MFS teacher, once noted, "rather than just teach them subject matter."

The sheer depth of the course offerings, sports opportunities, musical and visual arts productions, and extracurricular activities has expanded dramatically in the last 50 years—primarily through the efforts of innovative, imaginative educators in the '70s and '80s and more recently to ensure that MFS students are prepared to compete in today's highly charged, competitive academic arena.

MEMORY MILESTONE

I was painting a picture in kindergarten with a friend of mine at the little easel, with these little things of poster paint. We were doing these big pictures of houses, the house, you know, that everybody does, with the walk and the tulips, and the chimney sometimes off at an angle, one of those houses. I put a nice blue sky right across the top and my friend put her sky all the way down. I made a nasty comment, and Dorothy Durbin, our teacher, overheard and just quietly took me by the hand and we went over and I got up onto the window seat and looked out the window and I discovered all by myself that, in fact, the sky went all the way down. I always remembered it, and I think it's just a superb illustration of how to teach, how to help people learn it for themselves. It was a very nice way to help me see that I didn't need to be too quickly critical. It was a good lesson to learn.

—*Anne Wood '44, interviewed by Maeve Kelly '09, for Kelly's senior Capstone project*

These first-grade students may think they're enjoying some picture books in Teri Kaiser's class. But they're also developing a foundation for the future as the Lower School curriculum focuses on academic rigor and spiritual and ethical development. Learning is very hands-on, and teachers make every effort to ensure the subjects come alive.

In the Lower School, headed by Director Kelly Goula, students participate in an integrated program of reading, writing, language arts, mathematics, social studies, and science organized around diverse themes and student-initiated investigations. Learning is hands-on: subjects come alive as students read, write, ask questions, interview experts, conduct experiments, take field trips, and share their learning. Students are taught to think critically, which in a Quaker education

MEMORY MILESTONE

There was a sensitivity here, an awareness. There was a spirit. This was the turning point in my life.

—Christopher Hansen '50

The Suzuki violin program is an integral part of the second-grade curriculum.

means that they strive to gather complete information, be precise, develop a plan when solving a problem, and shift strategies when needed. Classes in visual arts, music, physical education, computers, library use, and Spanish complement the Lower School academic program.

Under Director Steven Shaffer, Middle School students take courses in major subjects of English, math, history, science, and world languages as well as courses such as woodshop, health, art, music, and physical education. Middle School students learn to use technology, to prepare for tests and papers, to organize themselves, and to participate in creating a strong Middle School community. Students may sing in the choir, play an instrument in the ensemble, or contribute articles to the Middle School newspaper. Beginning in grade six, boys and girls can compete on several interscholastic athletic teams in soccer, field hockey, basketball, lacrosse, tennis, and baseball.

Associate Head of School/Academic Dean Barbara Caldwell has been at the school since 1993. After serving as Chester Reagan Chair for Quaker and Religious Studies and then as Upper School director, she was appointed to her current position in 2004 overseeing the academic program and faculty.

Outside of the classroom, Middle Schoolers enjoy a number of field trips, including a trip to Mystic Seaport, Connecticut, in grade five and an outdoor education program at Stokes Forest, New Jersey, in grade seven. During the six-day Intensive Learning period, when each grade level devotes time to a special project, activities may range from learning about ancient civilizations to studying zoo design to executing all aspects of a theatrical performance.

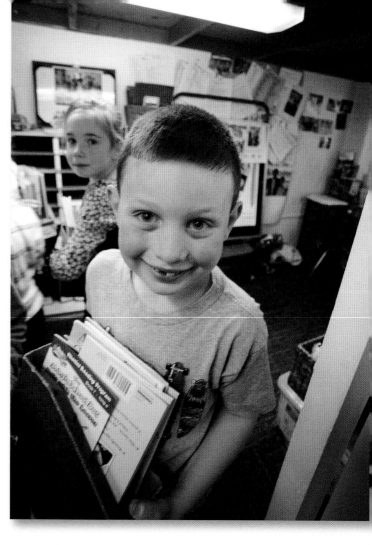

MEMORY MILESTONE

I really enjoyed the week of Intensive Learning each year. I had an experience that helped solidify my choice of career. When I was in 10th grade during City Project [learning about Philadelphia], Daan Calta (now Ze'ev Gilad) and I got lost going the wrong way down South Street. We were a little anxious and were talking about what to do. A blind woman happened to pass us and overheard our predicament. She stopped and asked us where we wanted to go. I thought she could not help us as she could not see, but I told her. She responded by telling us to go to the corner and get on the 41 bus, get off at the fifth stop and go two blocks north and we would be there. I was amazed when I realized she had a better mental map of the city than I could hope to have even with good vision. It made me realize being blind is not the end of the world. Vision adds a richness to our lives. I work to preserve that in children and adults every day as a pediatric ophthalmologist.

—*Mansoor Movaghar '87*

In the Upper School, the academic bar has never been higher—partly in response to the 2004 Strategic Plan that emphasized academic rigor. Led by Director Chris Kimberly, the curriculum offers students a broadly based liberal arts education, including sixteen Advanced Placement courses and honors-level courses in all major disciplines (including a 7:15 a.m. option for advanced organic chemistry; bring cups for hot chocolate). Critical thinking, strong writing skills, and quantitative reasoning skills are stressed at every grade level. Students can design their own course of independent study, and many explore subjects of special interest in significant depth, either through advanced courses or through a rich selection of electives. The relatively new MFS Honors Program emphasizes creativity, independence, and action for students who wish to undertake the most rigorous and wide-ranging curriculum the school has to offer.

Preschool teacher Patricia McEwan retired in 2010 after 14 years of teaching the school's youngest students.

The Bayshore Discovery Project, part of Intensive Learning, involves work on the A.J. *Meerwald* ship in Port Norris, New Jersey.

Classroom learning opportunities combine with action-oriented experiential activities. All students must complete 50 hours of community service, and many participate in service trips to locales such as New Orleans, the Florida Everglades, Mexico, Nicaragua, Costa Rica, and Tanzania. All students also participate annually in Intensive Learning, the weeklong off-campus collaborative educational experience. And because MFS students always seem to find the time, the school offers many sports annually (80 percent of Upper School students are on at least one team), and a rich theater program includes a fall musical and spring drama, as well as Drama Club and Shakespeare Club productions. Choir

Ashley Edwards '08 pictured with students during a service trip to Tanzania.

Chuck Blatherwick, a science teacher in the Middle and Upper Schools, takes a few moments to discuss matters with two of his students. The Upper School sciences at MFS cover biology, environmental science, chemistry, and physics, with Honors and/or Advanced Placement offerings in each. Elective courses contain material as varied as forensic science, robotics, and rocketry.

and Ensemble performance groups are also active, and students have the chance to join dozens of clubs that range from Operation Smile to Rocketry; from Japanamation to the BBQ Club; from Food Not Bombs to the Jewish Culture Club; from the Gay-Straight Alliance to the Future Business Leaders of America.

MEMORY MILESTONE

There we were—the members of Mr. Edgerton's Intensive Learning class—tumbling out of the yellow school bus in the middle of Philadelphia. . . . I remember being very impressed as we walked into the KYW newsroom. There was certain energy, a buzz, electricity that actually made my skin feel all prickly and ticklish. Then, we got to go into the studio and watched a live noon newscast. That was the first time I had ever seen a tele-prompter or green screen. . . . At the time, I had no interest in going into broadcast journalism. It was one of those experiences from which one looks back and wonders if that was "the moment." About fifteen years later, when I was sitting at the anchor desk in Indianapolis and welcomed Middle School students into the studio to watch a newscast, I couldn't help but remember Intensive Learning.

—*Linsey Davis '95*

Field trips have been a mainstay at MFS for decades, allowing students an opportunity to experience the real-life impact of their classroom lessons. Here, Middle School Director Steve Shaffer provides two seventh-grade students a closer view of plant life in Stokes Forest in mid-December 2008.

Choral concerts take place throughout the year. While some are formal affairs—especially in the Upper School—others are about vocalizing the lessons learned in the studio about pitch, harmony, and rhythm.

"The most important thing to me," said David C. Harris, School Committee member and the parent of Austin '13 and Hunter '17, "is to develop a love of learning, to go through life being curious, to not be afraid to be curious and to view life as a learning experience. That is never in doubt at Moorestown Friends."

The relatively recent addition of Advanced Placement and Honors courses caused some concern in the Quaker community, which emphasizes equality and

MEMORY MILESTONE

My overall experience with my Capstone project was a phenomenal one. . . . It's just so cool to think about the history of a place, and the people who have come before you. I used to love to look at the old yearbooks in the MFS library, too. I still do. For example, admission to the school used to be a couple dollars plus a share of firewood. I guess I've always loved that kind of history. . . . After the very first interview, I was obsessed. The MFS alums had such inspiring and fascinating stories to tell. In high school, we were all on separate paths and probably not thinking at all about who once sat at our desk or who shared our same seat in the auditorium decades earlier. MFS offered me the best high school experience I could have ever had. It's really hard to explain the community at school unless you've experienced it firsthand, but I will say that I felt as much a part of a family as I did a part of the high school community.

—*Maeve Kelly '09*

The MFS Robotics program extends from a Lower School Robotics club all the way up to high-level competition at the Upper School level. The team also leads many outreach activities with schools in Camden and Philadelphia. In 2009, the team participated in the FIRST Tech Challenge World Championships at the Georgia Dome in Atlanta, where they placed as semifinalists.

As dean of the Middle School, Maggie Ritchie Beck is charged with ushering four grades of students through a period of transition and discovery. Not only are the students gaining the skills and discipline to prepare them for Upper School, they are developing socially, emotionally, and intellectually.

Tina Wheaton Corsey, a Middle School science teacher and the Camden Scholars Program coordinator, explains a lesson to her class.

the strength of each individual but doesn't necessarily draw attention to different levels of achievement. However, the school administration and faculty pushed back.

"One of the issues that I have with Quakers is the idea that excellence is not something that Quakers do," said Associate Head of School and Academic Dean Barbara Caldwell, an experienced Quaker educator who in the 1990s was the third person to hold the Chester Reagan Chair. "Students can be excellent in any number of ways—excellent actors, excellent mathematicians, excellent athletes. One of our goals is to give them the opportunity to let that happen. On the academic side, that means we offer them the most rigorous curriculum that

Rehearsals get under way for the Lower School Spring Concert. In addition to winter and spring concerts, MFS stages several traditional shows such as *Goin' Buggy* (second grade) and *Rats!* (third grade).

The art show for the Middle and Upper Schools is a chance for students to display the efforts of all their work. The visual arts at MFS use a variety of media, including plaster, paint, clay, jewelry, fiber, and ceramics. Students take trips to major art museums to supplement their classroom learning.

we can offer. Everyone being on the same level is not what we are about. We should be able to reach down as well, and help the kids who are struggling, but you don't want to hold down the kids with the big capacities."

One thing has not changed, said Larry Van Meter, speaking as a former student and as head of school. Since MFS began, students have been encouraged to think for themselves, to ask questions. "In fact, this is very consistent over the years: to believe that questions are really more important than answers. Because so many things don't have clear answers."

MEMORY MILESTONE

My academic strengths were in mathematics and science, and my MFS teachers from kindergarten through 12th grade pushed me and empowered me. With Lower School computer teacher Donna Alley, I learned to design games and animations with the programming software LogoWriter. Mathematics department chair Michael Omilian helped me pursue independent study in trigonometry, geometry, and calculus while coaching me in the statewide Math League competition. The science department challenged me with Advanced Placement and laboratory courses, and it is thanks to this rigorous education that I excelled as a freshman at MIT. My proudest encounter with math at MFS, however, was as a young alumnus, running an algebra workshop for incoming Camden Scholars. This memorable experience allowed me to give back to the MFS community that had given me wonderful opportunities for so many years.

—*Tim Kreider '00*

5

Mentors from the classroom and the playing fields and courts, from early days to the present.

Teaching and Coaching Icons

The 1948 Moorestown Friends School faculty. Front row *(left to right)* Robert Taylor, Marjorie DeKlyn, Chester Reagan, Harley Armstrong, and Alfred Deyo; Second row: Helen Hersperger, Marguerite Cowan, Frances Bartley, Genevieve Hadley, Elizabeth Bushnell, and Anne Baldwin; Third row: Herman Magee, Joseph Lippincott, Cully Miller, LeRoy Darlington, and Wilbur Carr; Back row: Gwendolyn Coney, Helen Meader, Henry Edmunds, Polly Phillips, and Sally Stokes.

Celebrating 225 Years
of Quaker Education

One bore an uncanny resemblance to Abraham Lincoln and inspired political debate. Another quoted Scripture during a lesson on mathematical equations and taught a future Nobel Prize physicist to look beyond the treetops and into the sky. One rallied generations of lacrosse players with her saying, "If you can touch it, you can catch it," while a soccer coach taught young men how to win and still be gentlemen. And year after year, others inspired passions and changed lives through the magic of music, art, and theater.

A remarkable group of teachers and coaches at Moorestown Friends School have made lasting contributions to the entire school community. While singling out any teacher in a school known for its remarkable sense of community is always difficult, these larger-than-life faculty icons inevitably enter the spotlight, revered for both career-long excellence and for that one, unforgettable moment when they touched a student and learning happened.

Benjamin Franklin once said, "Tell me and I forget. Teach me and I remember. Involve me and I learn." With this statement, the prominent statesman unknowingly described the secret to a great faculty at MFS.

Teacher Martha Swan sits front and center of her class in the early 1900s.

The strength and dedication of the MFS teaching staff have rarely been questioned. The early faculty were "born teachers," Ruth Conrow Williams '14 liked to say, professional men and women known for what William C. Coles Jr. '22 often described as "strict standards and sound educational principles." For years after the two schools joined in 1920, third graders enjoyed Louisa M. Jacob's lively nature walks while Carolyn A. John, a noted watercolorist in the area, charmed students every time she put brush to paper. Martha C. H. Swan was a classroom disciplinarian both adored and sometimes feared by Lower School students. Robert M. Taylor, a physics and chemistry teacher from 1924 to 1959, faithfully taught the sciences to several generations of students, gradually accepting the nickname "Cube Root." Latin teacher Alfred Deyo was known for his quip, "No question about that!" and he always stood on stage to lead students in singing hymns during assembly. In addition to Latin and history, he drilled students on the finer points of writing and rewriting, helping to establish MFS's long-standing reputation as a school that teaches students to write well. Remembered one yearbook editor, "Mr. Deyo's room was knee-deep in torn papers after three hours of Senior Essay writing."

In 1926, Chester Reagan convinced Wilbur "Toddy" Carr and Herman Magee to join the faculty, the beginning of what was eventually known as "the Old Guard" at MFS, a team of dedicated, long-term teachers that also included David S. Richie '26, Harley Armstrong, and Jean Ricketts. Carr, a math teacher, class advisor, and assistant head of school during his 41 years at MFS, would not tolerate students being late to class, and often walked the halls to keep the student body in check. But beneath a rather stern exterior, he was a school spirit fanatic who loved the tradition of Color Day, Social Security Dances, the Friendship Fair, and every athletic event, including those coached by his colleague Herm Magee.

MEMORY MILESTONE

My six years at MFS were certainly the happiest of my childhood. One reason was the stimulating intellectual atmosphere encouraged, most memorably, by Cully Miller. He taught so much more than history to us. He encouraged debate about the key issues of the day. These included pro and con the Korean War, Senator Joe McCarthy, and each national election campaign. In effect, he brought the daily news to life and made sure his students understood both sides of each issue without leading us to a foregone conclusion. Our classes always represented both conservative and liberal viewpoints, many of which were heatedly debated but always with respect for the opposite viewpoint. This led me to focus part of my own career mediating international disputes in the Middle East. Every time I sat down with someone whose views were diametrically the opposite of my own, Cully's smiling face would pop into my mind, quietly whispering to me, "Listen to him, even if you completely disagree, and then try to find some middle ground where both parties to this dispute might find room to negotiate."

—Paul Mecray '56

English teacher Jean Ricketts enjoys a moment with her class in 1962.

When he wasn't teaching gym classes and the rather odd combination of calisthenics and marching tactics, Magee coached soccer, basketball, and baseball at MFS for 42 years, admonishing his young athletes to "play well, play fair, and play like a gentleman." An award named for Magee recognizing outstanding contributions to athletics is bestowed annually to a male and female athlete, while an award for dedication, excellence, and outstanding participation in girls lacrosse is given in honor of Florence "Floss" Brudon.

With her engaging smile and sense of fun, Brudon's pixie stature belied her towering presence at MFS. From the moment she walked on campus in 1949, Brudon endeared herself to generations of female athletes who still credit their active lifestyles and competitive edges to the skills they learned in Brudon's physical

Coaching icon Herm Magee (*hat*) addresses the 1948 soccer team at halftime.

The 2010 girls lacrosse team takes a break from an indoor practice on a rainy day.

education classes or on one of her many lacrosse, field hockey, tennis, and basketball teams. Known for her "If you can touch it, you can catch it" coaching axiom, Brudon is credited with introducing lacrosse to not only MFS but to South Jersey. In 1998, when she was inducted into the New Jersey Lacrosse Hall of Fame, a sportswriter noted, "If you've ever seen a high school lacrosse game in South Jersey, you can thank Florence Brudon. She is simply irreplaceable."

As a student in the late '50s and early '60s at MFS, Larry Van Meter recalls that the faculty "was wonderful. There were more Quaker teachers back then, but all of the teachers, as today, had a really good rapport with the kids. They were good scholars in their own right, but the quality of interaction between teachers and students is one of the things that really hasn't changed much in 40-plus years."

A "New Guard" had moved into place by the time Van Meter arrived, a

MEMORY MILESTONE

I remember Neil Hartman, a math teacher who also taught religion classes. One day in math class, he presented students with a particularly thorny problem that had us all struggling to find the answer. One wise-guy student in the class decided to call upon his Bible knowledge to get the solution. He called out to Mr. Hartman, saying, "Ask and it shall be given you," to which Mr. Hartman, without missing a beat, replied, "Seek and ye shall find."

—*Janet Sawyer Thomas '67*

Social Studies teacher Cully Miller connected students with the outside world and challenged them to think. He helped develop the first Mock Political Convention in 1960 and was one of the first teachers to use technology as a teaching tool.

group of formidable teachers such as Cully Miller, Neil Hartman, Sandy Heath, Warren Shelley, John Caughey, Ruth Sawyer, Victoria Starr, and Harrie Price.

An MFS teacher from 1946 until he retired in 1985, Cully Miller was the personification of Quaker idealism, political liberalism, and social activism—one of the first teachers, it could be argued, to think out of the box before the phrase became fashionable. More than anything else, the lanky teacher—who towered over most students and resembled Abraham Lincoln when he grew his beard—wanted students to think. Toward that goal, he gradually designed and taught history courses for a new trimester system: Conflict Resolution and World Order, Local Government and Politics, the Middle East, and Economics. He organized seminars to Washington, D.C., and took students to the United Nations in New York. In 1960, he helped develop

MEMORY MILESTONE

It seems a lot of my life achievements came from the influence that Floss Brudon had in my life. I can still hear her say, "If you can touch it, you can catch it!" Oh, how that statement made me try just a little harder to achieve my goals.

—*Mary McVaugh Shannon '71*

Students from the Class of 1972 work together on a senior project.

From an extensive book collection to an impressive online database collection, the MFS library is a prime resource for learning at the school.

the concept of a Mock Political Convention, where students in every grade could role-play each aspect of a political convention. He was one of the first teachers to use technology in teaching (microfilm, projectors, and slides) and was an accomplished photographer. And with the backing of Alex MacColl and the groundswell of innovation that surfaced in the early 1970s, Miller and a group of forward-thinking teachers like Sandy Heath and Ed Dreby started the City Project in 1973, a three-week intensive learning program for ninth and 10th graders to study the city of Philadelphia. The program was the genesis for the current Intensive Learning program, the school's signature experiential learning program for grades five to 12.

Miller mentored students as well as younger faculty members, including

Margaret Barnes Mansfield, an outstanding Middle School social studies teacher who ran four mock political events after Miller retired and embraced his ideas on experiential learning. Said Mansfield, "Instead of having kids learn about X, Y, and Z, they can see, hear, and feel the experience unfiltered. History is about interpretation. There is no one answer. I like to help kids find meaning in their life. A well-examined life is a wonderful life to live." As Miller sought to connect students with the outside world, MFS math teacher Neil Hartman strived to reconnect them to the richness within MFS. From

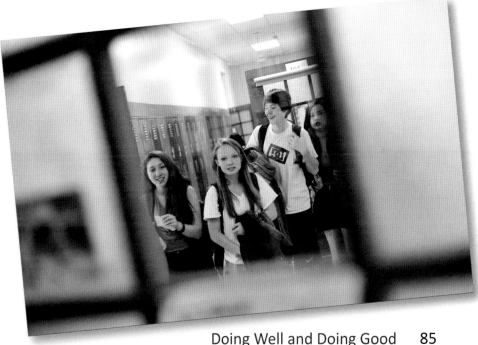

In the Lower School, the process of creating art is an important first step, no matter which media. Students' hard work culminates at the annual Lower School Art Show.

1952 until he retired in 1985, the relatively quiet and exceptionally dry-witted Hartman wholeheartedly supported MFS traditions like Color Day, Friendship Fair, and May Day, where he taught students the traditional May Pole dance every year. He was the school's first tennis coach in 1963 (he once advised the players to, well, "Hit it back!" when they asked him how to play, and they won two state championships in 1977 and 1978).

A staunch Quaker and conscientious objector during World War II, he participated with students in the March on Washington in 1963, and forever recalled the magic of hearing Martin Luther King Jr. speak. He was the first chairman of the school's Religious Life Committee, a group of students who met twice a month to discuss moral and social issues like war, peace, abortion, and interracial marriages. Hartman admits that some of the most difficult times at MFS were during the Vietnam War, when students interrupted Meeting for Worship to protest the war; Hartman understood the sentiment, but did not think the Meeting House was the right venue for protest. He witnessed the dawn of the computer age and was instrumental in getting the school's first computer in 1970. "I enjoyed computers and . . . it is the one thing in math class that you can count on our students enjoying."

MEMORY MILESTONE

Middle School social studies teacher Margaret Mansfield is—without question—one of the finest educators I've ever known. Her warmth and compassion made her classroom a profoundly welcoming place. Whether immersed in a compelling classroom discussion or venturing across the street to make a chalk-rub impression of an old headstone, Margaret always kept us thoroughly engaged. The gentle intensity of her commitment to social justice has stayed with me most clearly; I will continue to carry her example of graceful and passionate dedication to making our world a better place.

—*George Laufenberg, MFS student, 1989–1991*

Math teacher Neil Hartman was one of the "New Guard" of teachers when he arrived in 1952. He stayed at MFS for 33 years. Religious, quiet, and possessing a dry wit, Hartman's presence could be felt everywhere—from the tennis courts, where he led MFS to two state championships to the nation's capital, where he participated with students on the March on Washington to hear Martin Luther King Jr.

Hartman notes that he derives "tremendous satisfaction in what my former students have done with their lives. They include a college professor, a business bigwig, a president of a computer science company, doctors, and even the head of a local private school. I brag that I taught Joe Taylor, the Nobel Prize winner, how to identify trees. I told him to look up. And he went on to look further, into the sky, and became a physicist."

In recent decades, a new generation of outstanding teachers emerged at MFS, bringing their signature strengths to a school with a long history of teaching excellence.

Davie Weiner, an MFS parent of two, directed the Ensemble for 25 years, building the program from scratch. She started with three or four students in 1974 in a Lower School fifth-grade classroom "where they used to keep whale blubber," she remembered. "I'm not sure how long it took to cross Pages Lane, but I

Music teacher Davie Weiner spent more than a quarter of a century building the MFS Ensemble from the ground up. Starting the program in 1974, the Ensemble grew in size and stature, and her concerts were always a welcomed event. But some say that Weiner's real skill was the confidence she instilled her students. "She made everyone feel they were a wonderful musician," recalls one parent.

eventually had 32 kids in the Upper School, all flutes, with a few violins that I pulled in." Robert and Gwynne Edmund watched as Weiner taught their three daughters—Marisa '94, Genevieve '89, and Nicole '86 (now an art teacher at MFS). Said Gwynne Edmund, "They loved Davie." Added Robert Edmund, "She made everyone feel that they were a wonderful musician." When Weiner retired after her last spring concert in 2000, Richard Stouffer '02, a member of the Ensemble, orchestrated a farewell tribute to Weiner that included a surprise performance of "Through the Years" by Kenny Rogers, letters of appreciation, and a special scrapbook from former students. "A lot of the concerts were special because of the way the kids played," said Weiner. "But this one? This one was emotional because I was leaving, and they were saying good-bye."

Arts department chair Richard Marcucci tried to say good-bye in June 2009 after 30 years of teaching art, building the school's art major, creating an Advanced Placement studio program, and directing the school's theatrical program for 23 years—but he simply couldn't bring himself to completely retire. So in the fall of 2009, the semiretired artist returned to teach art history for Middle School

Arts department chair Richard Marcucci never saw the arts as painting, singing, or playing a musical instrument. To the 30-year veteran, the arts—both visual and performing—were disciplines that helped develop self-esteem and problem-solving skills, enhanced creativity, and boosted self-confidence.

students and an Upper School course called Art and Spirit, taught jointly with Priscilla Taylor-Williams. "I love opening up young minds to art and art history," said Marcucci. "The arts are not just a sideline. They are an opportunity for kids to sing and act or draw or play instruments. An art curriculum is essential for so many reasons—creativity, problem solving, certainly it helps develop self-esteem and helps students discover things they didn't know they could do. Art and theater have an inherent kind of quality and impact on lives. If I was able to make that more accessible, that thrills me."

Children who walk into Teri Kaiser's first-grade classroom are thrilled to find words on everything—the Word Wall, the back of a chair, on bookcases, on theme units for special areas of study. *Space, Astronaut, Shuttle, NASA.* "I use every inch of the classroom for words," said Kaiser, who first joined MFS as a kindergarten teacher in 2001 and began to teach first grade seven years later. "My favorite subjects to teach are reading and writing. I love the excitement of seeing the light go on when

Enter first-grade teacher Teri Kaiser's classroom, and you're visually immersed with the English language. "I use every inch of the classroom for words," says Kaiser, who came to MFS in 2001, and who considers reading and writing the lifeblood of academia. "You have to surround [the kids] with lots of literature, books, and words, and read out loud to them."

it all starts to connect. It's really empowering when you know you can read and write. Children get so excited about it, and you see all that growth happening during just one year."

Kaiser said that she and her Lower School colleagues constantly explore a variety of reading, writing, and math programs to develop best practices that "fit our students' needs. If one child isn't reading, I immediately think, 'How can I help?' Children reach reading in different ways. But I think that if you surround them with lots of literature, books, and words, and read out loud to them, they start to pick it up. And writing is vitally important because it's so connected to reading. The students start by expressing themselves with pictures and drawings, but they move on by listening for sounds and then stretching the word out and putting it on paper. And they can read it—even if it is in their own, unique spelling. It really is amazing."

After Kaiser's daughter Claire graduated from MFS, her college professors always told her that she wrote excellent papers, a trademark of an MFS education. And that skill, Kaiser believes, is developed in every Lower School classroom.

Mandarin Chinese language instruction began in 2008.

To refer to 20-year-veteran Michael Omilian as a math teacher and departmental chair at MFS would be a gross oversimplification. The school's computer system and network have his fingerprints all over them; he devises the complex Middle and Upper School class schedules; and the robotics team, theater stage sets, and student government all benefit from his assistance. As Omilian points out, a "teachable moment" can present itself at any time.

When Michael Omilian, MFS math department chair and teacher, spoke at the 2009 Commencement, he noted that "one of our goals at MFS is to give you a love of learning and an understanding that you need to be a lifelong learner to succeed in today's world." For the past 20 years at MFS, Omilian has tried to do just that—through sharing with students his own passions for mathematics (he teaches seventh- to 12th-grade math courses) and technology (he helped spearhead efforts to develop two computer labs, an integrated networking system, and a technology strategic plan), or simply lending a hand with robotics, student government, and set construction for student plays. But it's in the classroom where Omilian makes connections for lifelong learning that are absolutely seamless. Calculus? It's more than numbers; it's understanding how things change over time. To show this, Omilian makes a video of students running across the Oval; uploaded to the computer, the video is used to teach a lesson on finding instantaneous velocities by the slope of a line. "And while I may be teaching the slope of a line, kids will always come up with a question that is not on topic, but reflects what is happening in the news, or a dilemma they heard about in Meeting, or a personal conflict about an ethical choice. At MFS, we are a place where that gets recognized, where we embrace a teachable moment that is so much more than a lesson plan."

For Karen Washington, director of multicultural affairs and Upper School Spanish teacher, those teachable moments often come when least expected. She recalls the

Upper School Spanish teacher Karen Washington ensures that everyone's voice is heard at MFS, and not just in Spanish. As director of multicultural affairs, Washington balances a mini United Nations of cultural, racial, and socioeconomic backgrounds on campus. Through her efforts, this melting pot of diversity is a source of pride at Moorestown Friends School.

Barbara Kreider, PhD, can deliver hot chocolate in one hand and conduct a 7:15 a.m. advanced chemistry class with the other, but the mission is the same—to ensure that every student knows they can learn science. A former college professor, Kreider, chair of the MFS science department, says she "respects [the students'] desire to learn, and I am the one who is supposed to help make that happen."

Mock Political Convention in 1996, when fifth-grade students created a Confederate flag to hang in the gym to represent the state of Georgia; many of the 12th-grade students wanted it to come down, claiming it was a symbol of racism and not a traditional symbol like the other state flags. "It was emotional," said Washington. "Students were upset, parents were upset, but it became this teachable moment and the flag came down. People who didn't previously think they had a voice learned that they did."

And as MFS has continued to embrace diversity—through student enrollment, diverse school clubs, and SEED (Seeking Educational Equality and Diversity) training conducted by Washington—the school's embrace of both racial and socioeconomic diversity has become a source of pride for one of its most celebrated programs. "The Camden Scholars were previously quiet about the distinction, to help them acclimate to a different environment," said Washington. "But now? They celebrate it. They are proud of this tradition of success."

Celebrating earth sciences, chemistry, and environmental stewardship is one of the driving forces behind the work of Dr. Barbara Kreider, chair of the MFS science department since 1998 and the mother of three MFS graduates. A former college biology professor, she has strengthened and expanded the school's science program by recruiting outstanding teachers and establishing a more rigorous curriculum. She spearheaded the effort to incorporate more science throughout the Middle and Lower Schools, too. The award-winning teacher—who sprinkles her conversations with "Gosh darn," serves hot chocolate to students, and doggedly pursues science competitions for her students and staff—brings passion and an infectious teaching style to the classroom, including a 7:15 a.m. advanced chemistry class for students who can't otherwise fit it into their busy schedules. "I've never worked with anyone more determined to find new ways of helping students connect with science in general, and chemistry in particular," said science teacher Andrew Newman.

Kreider has her own teaching mantra. "Anyone can learn science," she said. "I find that if kids believe that *I* think they can learn, and if *they* think it is useful, everyone can learn. I'm not saying everyone is passionate about quantum physics, but they can learn it. And I just love listening to the kids, because they are so funny. That's part of it. You probably notice the kids call me by my first name—the respect comes from what's between my ears, not the name I'm given. In turn, I respect their desire to learn, and I am the person who is supposed to help them make that happen. I will teach as long as it's fun, as long as I laugh every day."

MEMORY MILESTONE

The day the violins arrived, the air was charged with excitement for us all. However, as the children took the violins out of their cases and held them upside down, backward, and any which way, my heart sank and I really thought that this time we had badly miscalculated. Not so. As lessons began, the daily acquisition of knowledge became a wonderful way not only for the children to begin playing violin but also for them to see a terrific example of study skills in action, of taking a small step each day to lead to a gigantic leap by the end of the year. . . . As the years have progressed, Marge Dawson and I developed such an instinctive feeling for the program that the instruction became more sophisticated. For Marge, having children lead the group and make up their own songs was special. For me, seeing the reaction of parents and friends to the children's playing at the May recital was priceless. The second-grade skills that are reinforced through this program are invaluable—listening, work, a sense of accomplishment.

—*Hazel Edwards, former second-grade teacher, recalling the moment in 1989 when the MFS second-grade Suzuki violin program began*

Student life is full of traditions— some serious, some quirky, and some just plain fun.

STUDENT TRADITIONS, HALLMARKS, AND FUN

The 1960 Mock Political Convention

CELEBRATING 225 YEARS
OF QUAKER EDUCATION

S tudent traditions are woven into every corner of the Moorestown Friends School campus—from greeting the Hippo on the first day of school to shaking hands with the head of school at Commencement on the Oval. Quirky, unique, and extremely fun student traditions have over the years helped MFS students distinguish themselves and grow as individuals within the framework of one school, one community. And make no mistake: everyone recalls a favorite MFS tradition. Here are some favorites.

Student Traditions

Meeting for Worship: Nothing requires less—and nothing gives back more—than this weekly, enduring tradition. With rare exception, MFS alumni recall Meeting for Worship as a gift, and continue throughout their lives to seek that same measure of quiet, reflection, and openness to the spirit that they first experienced as students.

In 1959, public schools in Prince Edward County (Virginia) closed rather than integrate, or desegregate, so consequently my brother and I were out of school; he was out of school two years, and I was out for one year. The American Friends Service Committee sent representatives to interview students who wanted to leave the area to finish their education. I was lucky enough to be placed with a family in Moorestown. I was chosen to go to Moorestown Friends School. There were seven of us. The rest of the students went to public school in Moorestown. It was a challenge at first, being the only black in the school except for the science teacher. Believe it or not, there were very few racial problems—I can't think of any incidents that were racial. I was accepted and treated very, very well.

—Sam Cobbs '62, *first African American graduate of Moorestown Friends School*

May Day: Some of the earliest school pictures document this joyful spring event that now takes place every four years, complete with a Grand Procession, dancing around the May Pole, beautiful costumes, a May Day Court with king and queen, and Shakespearean plays (only a few remember Molly Forsythe's stubborn cow).

Nature Walks, Field Trips, Class Trips: From the moment this Quaker school was built, students have been encouraged to get back outside. Early nature studies and bird walks evolved into traditional camping trips and overnight excursions for specific grades, including Camp Bernie in third grade, Mystic Seaport in fifth grade, Camp Dark Waters in seventh grade and more, with trips to D.C. and New York in Upper School. The Class of '27 was the first in the history of MFS to take a trip to Washington.

Exchange Programs: Originally known as the Affiliation Program, the international exchange programs with schools in France, Germany, and Japan have been a school tradition since the 1950s. Neil Hartman began the exchange program with Tokyo Friends in 1959; the MFS German exchange began in the early 1950s. Families like the Lippincotts have hosted multiple exchange students, and the Moriuchi family now counts two generations of the same family as part of their exchange experience.

Moorestown Friends School's exchange program dates to the 1950s. Whether wrapping packages to send to friends in other countries or welcoming those students to America, the program always builds relationships and better understanding between cultures.

I was honored by the school to serve as its exchange student to the Rudolf Steiner School in Nürnberg, Germany. Spending a year at age 16 in Germany was an unbelievable experience. When I returned, the Vietnam War was in full swing, and we had very lively debates in Meeting about how to stop it and how to liberate the school from many of its traditions, like short hair! Some of the exchanges were intense, but always respectful. MFS was a fantastic experience. I loved the teachers, particularly Jerry Delamater, John Caughey, and Grace Kennedy Blackburn, to whom I owe my entire career. We all have enormous potentials, but the marvelous thing about the Grace Kennedy Blackburns of this world is they make sure you see this fact of human life. My message to MFS students is this: No one can say what smart is. There is no scientific definition of smart. We all have tremendous potential, and we should never be discouraged by standardized tests or other people's opinions. None of us is standard, and creativity and initiative and luck can't be quantified. The faculty at MFS back in my day, as well as today, are incomparable because they realize that "all that's gold doesn't glitter" (Aragon, in *The Lord of the Rings*).

—*Larry Kotlikoff '69*

(Top photo) The May Day celebration dates to the earliest years of MFS, and little has changed in the decades since. With the May Pole dancing, beautiful costumes, and other events, it will no doubt remain a school staple for decades to come.

(Bottom photo) Seventh graders on an overnight field trip to Stokes Forest analyze water, minerals, and plant life in the local creek.

While the placements didn't constitute an "exchange," the American Friends Service Committee (AFSC) often placed international students at MFS during times of political and social upheaval. During World War II, MFS hosted a German Jewish refugee student named Peter Basch, while two "English girls" named Blanche and Louise Lawson attended MFS from 1940 to 1945 while living with the Wood family. Sam Cobbs '62 became the first African American student to attend and graduate from MFS when the AFSC selected him to join MFS in 1960, a year after schools in his native Virginia closed in protest over desegregation. And the AFSC is truly responsible for helping establish one of the most celebrated and enduring MFS legacies—the Moriuchi family. Takashi "Tak" and his wife, Yuri Moriuchi, who endured internment

MEMORY MILESTONE

When I was almost a senior at MFS, the fall musical was still being decided. I desperately wanted MFS to perform *Funny Girl*, and I did everything to persuade Mr. Marcucci to consider it—including a card with a list inside of the top 10 reasons why it would be a huge success for our school. Mr. Marcucci was a bit hesitant at first when he began to ponder what kind of undertaking a musical like that would be—I mean, there was tap dancing, big showy numbers, and a lot of dramatic acting involved. But Mr. Marcucci did what Mr. Marcucci does best—he took a risk and decided we would go for it. And it ended up being a truly memorable experience. I was convinced from then on to never give up on my dream. Mr. Marcucci is the person I will always remember who pushed me and encouraged me and lifted me up to be the best actor I could be. And I am so honored to have been in his company for the time I spent at MFS.

—*Lindsay Wolf '02*

and anti-Japanese sentiment in their native California, moved over 60 years ago to New Jersey through the help of the AFSC. More recently, in the 1990s, MFS partnered with a group called Community of Bosnia to place students from the war-torn country at the school.

Walking to Main Street: Senior privileges traditionally include time off campus, which begs for a traditional trek to Main Street. The Peter Pan Bakery with chocolate donuts and miniature cinnamon buns is gone, but there's always Starbucks and Passariello's.

Social Security Dances: Started in 1937, the Upper School Social Security Committee hosted one dance each month to inspire "social security" (the dances played off the name of the government's then-new Social Security program). The name was eventually dropped, but MFS still has dances, including the prom.

Senior Benches: Each Upper School class has a bulletin board, but only seniors have benches. It's understood: only seniors get near the senior benches.

Dress Like a Twin Friday and Hide Friends' Backpacks: No reason. Just fun.

Students make a wish at the 1964 Friendship Fair.

Friendship Fair: Every December starting in 1946, third graders rolled dates in sugar or stuffed them with nuts, sixth graders made wooden marionettes, parents canned jams and jellies, and Upper School students ran games, contests, and put on hilarious skits for the Friendship Fair, an annual event to raise money for the exchange programs between MFS and schools in Germany, Japan, and later France.

FAVORITE MEMORIES

Janet Thomas '67: *Scooting down the slide out the second-grade, first-story window during fire drill;* **Marguerite C. Cowan '41:** *Sugar-coated dates, Mr. Taylor's donut factory, and the wooden marionettes made by sixth graders at the Friendship Fair;* **Elizabeth Cooper Wood '40:** *Senior essay contests and extemporaneous speaking contests;*

Physical education in 1939 required special uniforms. Over the decades, the MFS program would grow to include many sports.

Harold E. Taylor '57: *Playing basketball in the old gym with the doors open to the auditorium so that we were on stage;* **Tim Kreider '00:** *Shakespeare Club and Monty Python Club, both proctored by English teacher John "Doc" LaVia;* **Ruth Stephen Barrett '29:** *Writing the school song, "Hail, All Hail the Red and Blue."* **Carolyn Kleiner '64:** *Sitting in the big window seats overlooking the buttonwood tree at the West Meetinghouse;* **Paul DiMaggio '67:** *Mock Political Convention, stumping for Henry Cabot Lodge, learning to "speak up and argue respectfully";* **Mustapha Khan '80:** *Organizing the first all-night MFS film festival in the West Building.*

Musicals and Theater: *Cranford, Fiddler on the Roof, Tom Sawyer, The Music Man, Grease, The King and I, Big, Joseph and the Amazing Technicolor Dreamcoat . . .* The theater arts tradition is grounded in the teachings of Jean Ricketts, Louise Morgan Geary, Beth Oliviero, Dee Bursch, Richard Marcucci, and Mark Gornto, who is a Middle/Upper School drama teacher. As Marcucci once said, there are very few weeks in the school year when the anticipation of auditions or the excitement and work of rehearsals is not present. The November musical includes students from grades eight to 12, and auditions begin in December for the winter play. Student-run productions are staged every spring.

The New Gym: Became *The Big Old Gym (The B.O.G.)*—and now it's the *Red Gym,* thanks to a refurbishment that included a new coat of red paint in 2009: Students love it, no matter what it's called.

Family Picnics: To strengthen the ties between Lower, Middle, and Upper Schools, the school has typically hosted family picnics after outdoor events like May Day and Color Day. The All-School Picnic is now a treasured tradition at the start of every school year.

The Hippo started as a fourth-grade art project in 1973 but has since become a lasting tradition at MFS.

Upper School girls enjoy the 2007 All-School Picnic. The annual tradition kicks off the school year.

The Hippo: The Hippo was created as an art project by fourth graders in 1973. In 1980, seniors decided to paint it during the dark of night, and the Hippo was suddenly reborn with a lavender base and pink polka dots. The late-night, paint-the-Hippo tradition was on. When the Hippo was damaged in 1980, Lower School art teacher Emma Richter gathered parents and students to rebuild the school icon, and it still exists. It's another school tradition to have your picture taken with the Hippo.

Second-Grade Strings: For the past 20 years, students in the second grade have started Suzuki violin instruction. For many, it's the first step in a lifelong musical journey, thanks to the innovation of former second-grade teachers Hazel Edwards and Marge Dawson.

MEMORY MILESTONE

Spirit Week is the one time where no matter what happened last week, we were a team. We had so much fun working together that it didn't matter if we won. I had never experienced anything like that prior to coming to MFS.

—*Cornell Woodson '05*

Spirit Week: For one week in October, the Upper School comes together for Spirit Week—a raucous, weeklong pep rally where students go all out to decorate hallways, perform air band skits, wear school colors, and win the tug-of-war contest.

Attending Moorestown Friends School is a family affair, and even grandparents get involved each year during the Lower School Grandparents Day such as this one in 2009.

Mock Primary Election, formerly Mock Political Convention: For just a moment, it's easy to forget that it's *not* a real convention—so convincing are the impassioned political speeches, the screaming delegates waving signs, the "security men" with black shades and dark suits, and the media representatives asking questions. This every-four-years tradition that began in 1960 provides political, social, and historical lessons that extend far beyond any chapter in a textbook. And it's been known to inspire a few political careers, too.

FAVORITE MEMORIES

Sanjay Bhatt, '07: *Thanksgiving Happening;* **Anne Wood '44:** *Being a snowflake on May Day;* **Carol Kiyo Moriuchi '71:** *Playing hours of soccer baseball in Lower School and then going downstairs to rest on those little blue cots, next to the boiler, while Mrs. Stiles would sit in the window well and read about the Dutch twins, Kit and Kat;* **Beth Freeland Clauss '81:** *The day Elisa Urbanelli recognized her as a new 10th grader and welcomed "new blood" into the class;* **Cornell Woodson '05:** *Spirit Week, playing Teen Angel in Grease, graduation on the Oval;*

William R. Archer '61: *Very good teachers, especially history;* **Whitty Ransome '63:** *the profound influence of Floss Brudon as a coach and friend;* **Rob Moose '00** and **Michael Rencewicz '00:** *Roaming the hallways, looking for a piano to play.*

The entire MFS community—including students, staff, faculty, and even alumni—enjoy taking part in the annual Thanksgiving Happening, such as this one from 2008, to create crafts and collect food for others less fortunate.

Thanksgiving Happening: This all-school event, started in 1991, mixes students from prekindergarten to 12th grade to create crafts and collect Thanksgiving food to give to others. Staff and faculty join in, and alumni often come back, too. Events culminate with mixed-age Meetings for Worship throughout the school.

Grandparents' Day: These special events are one big, continuous hug between students and their special friends and adoring grandparents.

Bricklaying and Quakerism: Ever since his son Brian '03 was in the second grade, Brent Schopfel has visited second-grade classrooms each year to help students understand how bricks are made and why they are so important to the Meeting House. The Quakerism unit also includes a Quaker Breakfast, with the students' own handmade muffins and crustless quiche.

Not all subjects have to be learned from books. For over a decade, alumni parent Brent Schopfel (pictured in 2009), president of Masonry Preservation Group, has visited second-grade classrooms each year to teach students about bricklaying.

MEMORY MILESTONE

In 2004, as a sophomore, I ran as Dennis Kucinich in the Mock Primary Election, competing against four seniors campaigning as other candidates. I decided to partici-pate as Kucinich because of his commitment to issues such as single-payer national health care and full-benefit gay marriage. I campaigned for two months,

Ben Spielberg '06 with 2004 presidential candidate Dennis Kucinich

making speeches, debating, and working with groups of students in grades five to 12. I was motivated and impressed by how much Kucinich's message resonated with other MFS students. Dozens of Middle Schoolers, even though they received no class credit for their work, signed on to help me promote Kucinich, designing posters while passing out and sporting Kucinich stickers, flyers, and gear.

On February 19, 2004, students from five different grades gave speeches on Kucinich's behalf in our full-day election. Kucinich won an easy victory as the school's preferred Democratic nomi-nee. After the primary, I contacted Kucinich's New Jersey campaign, became its high school coordinator, and eventually convinced the national campaign to bring Kucinich to MFS. When he visited on June 4, I made the speech introducing him. He inspired our student body with his vision of a society based on peaceful conflict resolution. I will always remember the Mock Primary Election and Kucinich's subse-quent visit as the highlights of my MFS experience, both because of the support I received from the community during my campaign and because of the strength of Kucinich's message.

—*Ben Spielberg '06*

Faculty, staff, and alumni take time to enjoy their meal at the 1979 Moorestown Friends School Lobster Dinner. The meal was renamed Dinner Among Friends and is held on Alumni Weekend.

Lobster Dinners, Clambakes: Started by social studies teacher and administrator Harrie Price on the first Saturday in June 1973, the annual MFS alumni gathering was an outdoor feast of lobster, steak, and clams. Price used to personally trek to Maine to purchase the lobsters. The tradition continued until the late 1980s. Today it has been resurrected in the form of the Dinner Among Friends on Alumni Weekend.

Intensive Learning Week: For one week each March, regular classes are suspended for "Intensive Learning," when Middle and Upper School students and teachers engage in an in-depth study of a specific subject, often involving off-campus research. This long-standing MFS tradition—which dates to the mid-1970s—allows teachers and students to break out of the structure of formal class periods and traditional study for a time of experiential learning in out-of-classroom settings. Students and teachers are freed to see themselves in a new light: as lifelong learners, students of the world around them.

MEMORY MILESTONE

In the fourth grade, I had the privilege of having Mr. George Thomas (Mr. T) as my teacher. The most noticeably different thing that year was sitting on the facing benches during Meeting for Worship. Wearing red socks on Fridays became commonplace, as Mr. T. kept track of who wore them consistently, even during our trip to Camp Ockanickon.

—*Chris Lloyd '05*

When MFS third graders make the trek to Camp Bernie, they're in for plenty of fun and challenges in the wilderness.

The 2010 fifth-grade trip to Mystic, Connecticut, was a chance to view, and experience, up close some of the most beautiful sailing ships in America.

Color Day: In a tradition that dates back to 1929, a student was either "red" or "blue" from the moment he or she entered school (for years, graduating seniors even identified themselves in the yearbook by the team color). Throughout the school year, the students staged academic and athletic contests between the Red and Blue teams (hare and hound chases, obstacle courses, shuffleboard, treasure hunts, and poster contests were all part of the fun), and tallied the points. The final day of competition at one time featured a parade with flags and cheering parents, faculty, and students, all before the final tug-of-war. The winners always celebrated, colors flying. In the 1970s, MFS abandoned the tradition, but Color Day is scheduled to return in the spring of 2011 as part of the school's 225th anniversary celebration.

FAVORITE MEMORIES

Leonard Green '32: *First president of the Varsity Club;* **Mary Ellen Avery '44:** *"Remember, if you ever see a turtle on a fence post, it didn't get there by itself!";* **Lisa Bobbie Schreiber Hughes '76:** *Building the one-room schoolhouse with Harrie B. Price during the school's Bicentennial;* **Martin C. Lehfeldt '57:** *The*

Time for reflection during Meeting for Worship

tolerance of different kinds of people and different viewpoints is essential to the building of a healthy society; **Anne Rosenberg '74:** *Miss Cowan for art with days on the lawn by the Meeting House to do watercolors, the wonders of chemistry with Mrs. Barbara Irwin, and spring classes outside on the Oval or under the tree;* **James A. S. Muldowney III '90:** *A second-grade report project on diabetes, the moment he decided to become a physician;* **Jim Bonder '96:** *Michael Omilian's style of teaching, Senior Project;* **Jamie Oliviero '68:** *The peace of Meeting and the time to grow.*

7

Students are supported by an active parent body, visionary trustees, and alumni who stay connected.

SCHOOL COMMITTEE, PARENTS, AND ALUMNI

The Moorestown Friends' High School faculty and School Committee, 1886.

CELEBRATING 225 YEARS
OF QUAKER EDUCATION

Red Sock Run 2007

Toward the end of the first act in the 2009 MFS fall musical, all 40 student actors are on stage, singing their hearts out. *Go, go, go, Joseph, you know what they say, Hang on now, Joseph, you'll make it some day!* This moment of sheer energy comes to life because in addition to these on-stage actors, at least 20 more students work behind the scenes, adjusting props, lighting, and sound; arts chair Brian Howard leads the ensemble that plays the music; over a dozen volunteer parents and staff like Rose Frola, Kiyo Moriuchi '71, and Kathy Tate provide costume, makeup, and hairstyling assistance backstage; the stage crew, led by the handy and talented Ben "Buck" Smith '10, has constructed the elaborate set.

Alumni lacrosse players and former coaches gather in 2008 to celebrate the 50th anniversary of the MFS lacrosse program. The program, started by Florence "Floss" Brudon, was one of the first in South Jersey.

For director Mark Gornto, it's one of his favorite moments in the play. "It's a big number, and everyone is on stage," said Gornto, an eight-year drama faculty veteran who posted audition sheets on bulletin boards before school even started. "The kids were wonderful, and there was tremendous support from students and parents, and it just says so much about the school. It's a fantastic feeling."

In many ways, the all-school production of *Joseph and the Amazing Technicolor Dreamcoat* holds up a mirror to what it really takes to operate a school like Moorestown Friends. In order to pull back the curtain and let the daily performance of operating a school begin—to swing open the front door of Stokes Hall and hear receptionist Doris Wilson say hello—the school depends on so much more than the 700 students and 100-plus faculty and staff who daily take center stage. In truth, MFS relies on the devoted spirit, diverse expertise, considerable time, and the resources of an entire backstage community—one that includes School Committee members, parents, and alumni.

MEMORY MILESTONE

Being an alumnus of MFS means much more than having a diploma with nice calligraphy. It means having memories of inspired teachers and incredible friends. It means being taught about the world and its inhabitants as a chain, and in doing so, awakening our social consciousness and making us responsible for the peace and change we wish to see in the world.

—*Sonia Mixter Guzman '02*

MEMORY MILESTONE

In regard to the buildings and grounds, every teacher and student deserves a nice place to spend two-thirds of their day. Heck, we spend more time here than in our own homes.

—*Jim Bottomer, Maintenance Department*

Since it first opened in 1785, MFS has been "under the care of the Meeting," originally known as the Chester Preparative Meeting of Friends but now called the Moorestown Monthly Meeting. A School Committee has always governed the school, reflecting a Quaker educational tradition. In 1920, the first year that MFS combined from two earlier Quaker schools, the School Committee involved 38 members, all Quakers; today, the School Committee includes up to 21 members, but only a majority of the members must be Quakers.

The amount of School Committee input sought by various heads of school has varied over the years, depending on the style of the headmaster and the difficulties facing the institution. By the late 1980s, the School Committee was very involved with running the school when leadership was in flux. When new head of school Alan Craig took back ownership of daily operations in the early 1990s, the School Committee's relationship with the school seemed to change forever. Said Tom Zemaitis, School

Emmy Award-winning filmmaker Mustapha Khan '80 visited campus in 2005.

Committee member and former clerk. "In the late '80s, early '90s, the School Committee was in transition. We used to have a very large committee composed of strictly Quakers, some who had no direct connection to the school. Alan's coming was a signal change. The change in the focus of the School Committee was to get members who were looking at the school for the future, not the day-to-day. It was a long, slow process."

In the last several years, the School Committee has worked in concert with the school administration to develop and execute a strategic plan built on the twin pillars of academic excellence and spiritual and ethical growth. The School Committee and administration have made bold plans to address a range of critical issues—raising faculty salaries (to compete with peer schools), increasing the financial aid budget to $2 million (27 percent of students receive financial aid), increasing the diversity of the student body and the faculty, implementing the new Honors Program and adding Advanced Placement classes, and purchasing nearby properties to help solve the school's growing need for more classrooms.

The Class of 1970 celebrated their 40th Reunion at Alumni Weekend 2010.

School Committee member Mark Mitchell '86 is vice president for school information services for the National Association of Independent Schools.

Gradually, the composition of the School Committee has changed to reflect the challenges of operating in a volatile economic climate. Today, attorneys, educators, entrepreneurs, and CEOs are among the ranks of the School Committee membership. Each of the members of the School Committee is dedicated to providing time, financial support, and expertise to the school. Indeed, each is asked to make a stretch gift to support the school's annual giving and capital campaigns, reflecting the School Committee's belief that it is important for its members to take a leadership role in fund-raising for the school.

William Guthe, the School Committee clerk since 2002, ultimately believes that the recent shifts in the School Committee reflect the complex reality in running an institution with a multimillion-dollar budget, considerable real estate holdings,

MEMORY MILESTONE

Moorestown Friends School and Edmund Optics Inc. Combine Resources to Support 10,000 Katrina Victims in Houston-Area Schools

Students, parents, staff, and faculty at Moorestown Friends School in Moorestown, New Jersey, have joined forces with Edmund Optics Inc. in Barrington, New Jersey, to expedite the delivery of needed school supplies to thousands of school children recently relocated from the Gulf Coast to the Houston, Texas area. . . . Students, parents, faculty and staff have collected more than 40 cartons of school supplies including calculators, pens, pencils, notebooks, crayons, folders, and construction paper. The MFS community also has collected donations for the American Red Cross. The money is being raised through donations and through a wide range of Upper School fundraising activities, including a breakfast, a pajama day, and a decision to donate the proceeds from an upcoming dance to relief efforts. Edmund Optics has also pledged $10,000 to the Red Cross and is matching all employee contributions to the effort.

—*September 20, 2005, newspaper article*

Photographed at the kickoff of the Campaign for Arts, Athletics, and Endowment in 2001 are: Joseph Young, Elizabeth Young, Emma Baiada '10, Diane Baiada, Anne Baiada, Caitlin Baiada '06, and Mel Baiada. Mel and Diane Baiada gave the largest single gift in the school's history, $3 million, to support the campaign that provided funding to build the Field House and renovate the Arts Center.

and more than 125 employees serving several hundred families and students. Explained Guthe, "In some ways, we had gotten complacent, and we didn't realize how we, as board members, needed to lead in terms of fund-raising. You have to show that the School Committee is leading."

Throughout the school's history, parents, alumni, and School Committee members have helped the school to grow in important ways. In the early years, families provided land for the school grounds and fields. As the need increased for improved facilities—as well as a permanent endowment—the school community has supported annual giving efforts and numerous capital campaigns to raise the money to meet these challenges.

Over the years, families such as the Baiadas, DeCous, Dillers, Enis, Matlacks, Moriuchis, Stokeses, and Yinglings led drives that transformed the physical campus and allowed MFS to meet the needs of its expanding academic and athletic programs. During these campaigns, the school realized a new gymnasium and renovated classrooms, a permanent endowment for Quaker education that's now worth over $1 million, Stokes Hall, the new Dining Hall Commons, the new Field House, many new endowed funds and scholarships, the complete renovation of the Arts Center, and a renovated Diller Library, designed to support the new technological and advanced computer resources the library now offers to students and faculty. In 2001, Mel and Diane Baiada gave the largest single gift in the school's history:

MEMORY MILESTONE

I was clerk of the School Committee, and Lydia Stokes wanted to help Moorestown Friends in our capital campaign. She was a Babbott before she married Emlen, and their kids were all alumni of the school. She was very generous, and she loved to build buildings. But we had one problem—we had a public road, Pages Lane, that one person down the lane had rights to, and we could not build the new building until we closed the road and figured this out. I spent well over a year in negotiations with Norman Oliver so that we could build the bloody building! We gave him access to his house for his lifetime, and we would keep Pages Lane open for him. The vestige of that road is still there, barely, straight out through the athletic fields.

—*Louis R. Matlack '53, clerk of the School Committee when Stokes Hall was built in 1986*

$3 million to support the Campaign for Arts, Athletics, and Endowment.

The campaign provided resources for the new Field House and the renovation of the Arts Center. "These new facilities will shape our children and generations of children to come," said Mel Baiada, during the Field House ribbon-cutting ceremonies. "Together, we have left an indelible mark on the history of Moorestown Friends School."

MEMORY MILESTONE

There is always a lot of confidence from the board in management, but we are fully cognizant of the challenges. During some recent discussions, the Quaker process nearly broke down, or it was perceived to have broken down. One of our challenges as a committee is to refocus on the Quaker process, to have open discussion, frank discussion, and come to a consensus, which we did. This actually brought the Quaker process back into focus.

—Mel Baiada, alumni parent and former School Committee member

Each year, the MFS community of parents and alumni also supports the school in ways that have nothing to do with writing checks.

Parents give their time and energy to support hundreds of sports events, orchestral and choral productions, field trips, student presentations, classroom activities, the MFS Thrift Shop, exchange programs, and academic competitions. They work in the Library, support Admissions Open Houses, run the Auctions, cheer from the sidelines, help build sets for and produce student plays, spend hours making beautiful costumes for those plays, help plan the Martin Luther King Jr. Day of Service, host the Camp Fair, and participate in the Red and Blue and Bravo! clubs. They supervise homework, help their children get through PSATs, SATs, and AP tests, and develop friendships that last long after their children have graduated. Family businesses often come into play, as parents and alumni have been known to donate everything from T-shirts to science equipment, give tours of orchards and farms, and visit MFS to discuss how bricks are made or how biological and financial challenges impact the search for a cure for AIDS. And sometimes the parents remain long after the students. "I've been

School Committee Clerk Bill Guthe, pictured with wife Carol "Kiyo" Moriuchi '71 and youngest son Geoffrey "Yas" Guthe at 2010 Commencement.

Doing Well and Doing Good   113

At the 2010 MLK Jr. Day of Service, parents got as involved as the students.

part of this community for over 20 years, and the youngest of my three sons graduated in 2002," said Lower/Middle School Quaker education teacher Lynne Brick, who initially began as a parent volunteer in 1986 before she was hired in her current position. "My connections to the school are as strong as ever. The bonds formed throughout this community are unique."

The school's 3,400 alumni are an equally dedicated and diverse bunch. With a list of accomplishments that include a Nobel Prize, an Academy Award, an Olympic Silver Medal, Emmy Awards, and a Holberg Prize, as well as celebrated careers in medicine, business, science, art, drama, teaching, academia, and writing, they regularly come back to the campus for reunions and quadrennial events like Mock Primary Election or May Day as well as various yearly functions like alumni soccer and basketball games and Alumni Weekends. Each year, distinguished alumni help welcome new scholars into world language honor societies and the Cum Laude Society for academic excellence. Beginning in 2000, the Alumni Association decided to honor accomplished alumni who have made significant contributions to their professions and communities while maintaining close connections with MFS. Toward that goal, the school now presents the Service Award, the Alice Paul Merit Award, and the Young Alumni Award.

The first Young Alumni Award was presented in 2006 to Sarah Adelman '96,

MEMORY MILESTONE

I am grateful to MFS for exposing me to Quaker values, for encouraging my interest in music and painting, and for providing me with the ability to write in an organized and thoughtful way, the latter having served me well throughout my legal career. I give to MFS so that future generations may have the same experiences and opportunities that I had. It is but a small thank-you for what the school gave me for 12 years of my life.

—Pat Metzer '59

now an assistant professor of economics at Mount Holyoke College, who combined stellar academic achievement with a commitment to global change in her first 10 years after graduation. A Phi Beta Kappa graduate of Stanford University, she received a degree in human biology, concentrating in population studies and sustainable development, before heading to the University of Maryland to pursue a PhD in agricultural and resource economics, with field work in northern Uganda on the quality of social networks and the impact of the civil war. At the MFS Young Alumni Award presentation, teachers recalled Adelman as a young student deeply committed to Quaker values and community service. A National Merit Commended Scholar, she brought analytical questioning to all of her MFS studies, whether examining ecological economics, dissecting frogs, or analyzing Kierkegaard. But it was her Commencement speech in 1996 that left few to doubt that Adelman would soon work to change the world. Moorestown Friends, Sarah Wallace Adelman said at graduation, had prepared her to "swing in the air . . . to let go, not to risk life, but to fly in it."

Alumni Service Award winner Bill Diller '59 (seated second from right) was joined by family and friends at the 2009 Dinner Among Friends.

MEMORY MILESTONE

The school had never won a state soccer championship before, and a lot of my very good friends were seniors. I clearly wasn't the strongest player, but part of a team-oriented, competitive, and caring group of people. We played a school that was five or six times our size at the time, and you just don't get to that place without a lot of people participating in the journey. For me personally, it was a heartfelt, wrenching time—it was the only game my parents ever went to, I had just recovered from mono, I was wiped out, it was our second overtime and I didn't even realize what had happened. I saw the ball in the net, and I remember thinking, "That can't be right, that has to be a mistake," and then the whole team is out on the field, carrying me away. It was honestly so much more about us winning than about me kicking the ball for the winning goal. And I think it highlights one incredibly important aspect of Moorestown Friends: everyone gets to have a moment like that. It might be a moment in sports, a moment for someone who is a Commencement speaker or the lead in a school play, a moment for someone who is a leader in an Intensive Learning capacity. MFS offers the opportunity for an individual to have his or her individual moment to shine. And I don't ever want us to lose that.

—*Ken Zekavat '80, parent and School Committee member, remembering the 1979 state championship soccer game*

Conclusion

At its 225th anniversary, Moorestown Friends School is stronger than it has ever been in its history. With a solid enrollment, a dedicated faculty, and Quaker values woven throughout its academically challenging curriculum, the MFS leadership has embraced the steps necessary to make a good school great while remaining true to its driving principles to provide personal, ethical, and spiritual growth for every student.

From this strong benchmark of success, MFS now faces a new canvas of challenges, similar to ones confronting nearly every Friends school across the country. What does it mean to be a Friends school in the 21st century? What does it mean to try to uphold and teach Quaker values within a school community where Quaker teachers are in a minority and Quaker students represent less than 5 percent of the student body?

These issues are being widely discussed not only by regional and local Quaker school educators but also by members of the Friends Council on Education (FCE), a national organization based in Philadelphia that provides support and guidance to its 82 member schools. As clerk of the FCE committee that evaluates schools for inclusion under the Friends Council umbrella, Larry Van Meter is well aware of the educational issues of "the post-Quaker world—that time, say, in 25 or 50 years, when conceivably the Religious Society of Friends is so diminished in numbers and influence that it isn't providing the guiding light that it did 50 years ago."

Granted, the decline in the "Quaker numerical presence," as author William H. Kingston III once called it, is not an altogether unfamiliar issue to Moorestown Friends; the decline in Quaker enrollment has been occurring for decades. But the issues facing today's Quaker school leaders are mostly without precedent, and are largely tied with steep drops in the number of Quakers in South Jersey and the Philadelphia area. How can Quaker schools be expected to promote Quaker education in and for a community where there are fewer and fewer Friends to lead the way?

For Van Meter and the leadership of MFS, the answer to this question can be found in the hallways, in the classrooms, on the playing fields, and in the Meeting House at MFS. "We have been and we will continue to be much more intentional about Friends' values and the universality of those values," said Van Meter. "It is a very deliberate part of the program and part of the religious studies that we have here. Through our sustained efforts to instill the Quaker message and values in all that we do, our students come out with a clear understanding of what Quakers believe, what they value. And we find that people are seeking out Friends' schools not just because they provide excellent academic opportunities but for that 'something else'— that Quaker dimension. Even in a potentially post-Quaker world, we are positioned to reflect, teach, and champion those values in a very genuine way. Although Quakers now constitute a small portion of the student body, the school's commitment to Friends' principles is as great—and perhaps greater—than it was 40 years ago."

The process of remaining quintessentially Quaker is something that means a great deal to John Caughey, former science department chair who taught for 23 years at MFS before retiring in 1986. "I actually think the school is more Quaker now than it used to be," said Caughey, a resident of nearby Medford Leas who still joins MFS students on the Meeting House benches for weekly worship. "The Chester Reagan Chair has done a lot to promote that, and Larry, himself a Quaker, is another example. But one thing that stands out is that they actually provide training today for what it means to be a Quaker, and they do a lot of teaching about Quakers before they go to Meeting. The students are certainly more worshipful during Meeting than they were when I was a teacher. We used to bring them over and tell them to be quiet, but now, through the efforts of the religion teachers, they are respectful of other people's feelings, of others getting something out of Meeting. I think there has been a genuine change from just sitting there and trying to keep quiet. Today, they understand the 'why.'"

In an era where strong, principled leadership is clearly needed in every financial, political, medical, and personal arena, Van Meter firmly believes that independent schools are especially well-suited to define and promote ethical leadership. "It's no accident," Van Meter wrote in a newspaper editorial in 2009. "Independent schools are free to define their own curriculum and to establish their own standards for teacher and student excellence." And, he pointed out, "Independent schools are free to teach ethics and morality in a way that is not permitted in public schools. In Friends' schools, the curriculum encourages students to be spirit-led and to think critically and behave morally—to be good citizens and neighbors in a popular culture that can be corrosive and that has far too much emphasis on selfishness. Now, more than ever, young people who are well-educated and who have values of the highest order are needed to provide leadership for a better tomorrow. We are fond of saying that we produce graduates who have a 'tough mind and a tender heart'—students who will not only do well in their chosen profession, but who also will do good for others."

As head of school, Van Meter works constantly to steer the school forward without losing what makes it special. With the School Committee's backing, Van Meter eagerly anticipates renovating the Greenleaf property, connecting the main campus with this former Quaker retirement facility. The expansion plans will help resolve a major classroom shortage at MFS and help protect what Van Meter calls "one of the hallmarks of MFS—the connection that students have with their teachers." When MFS acquired the Greenleaf in 2008, it was one of a half-dozen nearby properties purchased over several years by the school. The nearly $10 million real estate acquisition program raised some initial concerns but was clearly designed to help ensure that MFS continues to have the space needed to grow and meet the needs of its student body well into the future.

The question of size is a critical one in Quaker education, which prides itself on low student-faculty ratios and individual attention. Former

In 2008, MFS purchased the adjacent Greenleaf Retirement Community property, providing potential space for classrooms and laboratories. Coincidentally, a former resident of the Greenleaf was Alice Paul, who graduated from the school in 1901 and was a famed leader of the women's suffrage movement.

Priscilla Taylor-Williams, the Chester Reagan Chair for Religious and Quaker Studies, addresses students prior to Meeting for Worship.

teacher and track coach Sandy Heath, who still substitute teaches at MFS after retiring in 1999, wrote his PhD dissertation at the University of Pennsylvania on "The Effect of School Size on the Social and Psychological Development of Students." Said Heath: "There are large benefits to being in a small school, knowing everyone, being small enough that kids are still needed to be on teams and yet big enough that you have a lot of activities. We talk at MFS about academic rigor and ethics as the two tiers, but I consider size to be a third tier. School size determines the culture of camaraderie, of joy. When I substitute, it is rare that anyone is absent. The kids are tremendously happy."

Van Meter believes that MFS's current 700-student body is a good size, and he points out again that the property expansion drive is designed to "serve the needs of the school's current enrollment," not an expanded one. But Van Meter admits to being intrigued by the historical dilemmas of change vs. staying the same. When he looks around the campus, he is aware that Moorestown—the area's original rural, farming landscape and the school campus—has changed profoundly over the years. Land once devoted to farming has turned into residential developments, estates, and nearby shopping malls, and the former one-room school now commands multiple buildings on 48 acres. Yet Van Meter appreciates that essential elements of both the small town and the school have remained unchanged. First described as a "town of homes" by writer James Purdy in 1886, similar descriptions of Moorestown have persisted over the years. The *Moorestown News* in 1930 called Moorestown the "Residential Town of Distinction," and *Money* magazine in 2005 called Moorestown the best place to live in America, with an emphasis on its small-town appeal. "The historian—and alumnus and native Moorestonian—in me finds that both fascinating and reassuring," Van Meter said, pointing out that the touchstones of academic rigor,

spiritual growth, and individual attention are still very much in evidence at MFS, just as they were when the school began. "It's not inconceivable that 25 years from now, schools like MFS will need to be larger to be viable. But I hope that doesn't happen, because I think we are just the right size now."

In a perfect future, MFS will continue to be the school where former Camden Scholar Mark Mitchell '86 can still find the wooden plaque painted with his individual track records hanging over a doorway. It will still be the school where science department chair Barbara Kreider believes "every child is honored, where every individual is noticed and celebrated because we are small and we care and we create paths for them to be whatever they want to be." It will still be the same school where prekindergarten teacher Lisa Thomas Martin '84 can walk down the hallway and say, "That was my math room, I had English there, and I played hockey and lacrosse on those fields." It will still be the school where Cynthia Eni Yingling '75 watched three sons—Christopher '05, Timothy '09, and Gregory '11—be "transformed into well-spoken, well-written, and extremely driven adults." It will still be the school that gave Camden Scholar Cornell Woodson '05 "a gift of hope, optimism, and courage because I never thought that I would graduate from high school, let alone go to college." And it will still be the same school, said Karen Washington, director of multicultural affairs, "where people are comfortable where they are, but they lean into discomfort. Because if we don't get those probing questions, those introspective questions, we don't really go anywhere, do we?"

More than anything else, Moorestown Friends School will always be the school where each student can find a moment to shine. Where asking questions is as important as finding answers. Where graduating seniors are prepared to "swing in the air, not to risk life but to fly in it." Where the words "community" and "ethical" are part of the mission statement. Where every student understands the words of Quaker founder George Fox, whose message resonates throughout MFS and, more importantly, in the consciousness of students long after they have walked these hallways:

"Let your lives speak."

ALUMNI ASSOCIATION AWARDS

The Moorestown Friends School Alumni Association recognizes individuals annually at Alumni Weekend via three awards:

SERVICE AWARD

Through unselfish interest, loyalty, or personal commitment, Alumni Association Service Award winners enhance the quality of life in the Moorestown Friends School community through volunteer work, contributions, or other ways.

ALICE PAUL MERIT AWARD

Award winners fulfill one or more criteria:

- An individual who exemplifies the best qualities of MFS, including honesty, integrity, fairness, a commitment to serve others, and a dedication to equality and justice.
- One who uses his or her education from MFS or affiliation with MFS and gives of himself or herself to make the world a better place.
- One who has achieved a standard of excellence in one's chosen endeavor or field.
- One who has made significant contributions to his or her community, whether it is Moorestown or the community in which he or she lives.

YOUNG ALUMNI AWARD

This award may be made to a recent Moorestown Friends School graduate on or before the Tenth Reunion, who has distinguished him/herself either through meritorious achievement in the early years of his/her career, or through exceptional service to the community or to the school.

Alumni Service Award
2000: Marguerite "Peg" Cowan '41
2001: Florence "Floss" Brudon
2002: G. Macculloch "Cully" Miller
2003: Louis Matlack '53
2004: Neil Hartman
2005: John Caughey
2005: Cynthia Eni Yingling '75
2006: Takashi "Tak" Moriuchi
2007: Dudley "Sandy" Heath
2008: Warren Nelson '58
2009: William Diller '59
2010: Carmela "Connie" Muldowney

The Alice Paul Merit Award
2001: Alice Stokes Paul, Class of 1901
2001: James Scott '54
2002: Joseph Taylor Jr. '59
2003: Kenneth Mayer '68
2004: Mary Ellen Avery '44
2005: Mustapha Khan '80
2006: Lisa Bobbie Schreiber Hughes '76
2007: Thomas Hedges III '67
2008: Elizabeth "Whitty" Ransome '63
2009: Anne Rosenberg '74
2009: John Stubbs '54
2010: Christian Hansen '50

Young Alumni Award
2006: Sarah Adelman '96
2009: Brian Weaver '99
2010: Meruka Gupta Hazari '00

CUM LAUDE SOCIETY

The Cum Laude Society is a national honor society for independent school students. Students are selected for membership based on their cumulative record of academic excellence in all subject areas. No more than 20 percent of a school's senior class may be selected, with no more than 10 percent chosen during their junior year. Moorestown Friends School received its Cum Laude charter in 1962. Names appear as they were at time of induction.

1963
David Campbell
Ross Corotis
Patricia DeCou
Virginia Howitz
Lonna Kane
Patricia Loney
Sarah Mahler
Richard Mason
Kathryn Taylor
Louisa Wright

1964
Carolyn Buckwalter
Peter Deutsch
Arthur Goldberg
Bonnie Greenfield
Phoebe Lewis
Peter Reagan
Beatrice Sanborn
Gregory Wilcox

1965
Marion Bowman
Frank Cheney
Rolf DeCou
Nancy Denbo
Seth Kane
Martha Mechling
Fred Moriuchi
Elizabeth Reagan
Laurentine Richards
Thomas Roberts
Paul Sirotta
Howard Wildman

1966
Barry Ford
Julia Forsythe
Scott Kelemen
Susanna Lewis
William McDaniel
Sally McVaugh
Deborah Ohler
Nancy Roberts

1967
Robert Abramowitz
Margaret Brunt
Paul DiMaggio
Robert Gale
William Gardiner
Ralph Graham
Diana Harrison
Debora Lilly
John McKeon
Robert Reagan
James Taylor

1968
Anna Lee Berman
Craig Cosden
David DeCou
James Hunt
James Kelemen
Marc Levin
Kenneth Mayer
Linda Sieg
Dale Van Name

1969
Mai-Li Dong
Carol Forsythe
David E. Good
Christopher R. Hilbert
Laurence J. Kotlikoff
John Thomas Reagan
Donald Riviello
Steven W. Suflas

1970
Laurie Barnett
Debra Corley
Allan Doane
Miriam Fisher
Barbara Gardiner
Steven Poliakoff
James Riviello
Kathryn Taylor
Linda Van Name

1971
Seth Cohen
John J. Donnelly III
Bruce J. Franklin
Sheila Gin
Alexander H. Knisley
Diane P. Michelfelder
Michael B. Poliakoff
Lisa B. Silverman

1972
Steven A. Benner
Debra L. Harding
George P. Johnson
Charles W. Martin
Nancy E. Ohler
Melanie B. Oliviero
John R. Scattergood
Clare Stokes
Jane A. Taylor

1973
Robert Barnett
Lynn Foord
Kevin Kelly
Richard Kennedy
Walter Kornienko
Claire Miller
Nancy Chiyo Moriuchi
Robert Rosenthal

1974
Mark Bisbing
Margaret Caughey
Scott Franklin
Karen Kaufman
Sophia Koropeckyj
Anne Rosenberg
Kenneth Weisner

1975
Robert Caughey
Joan Craig
Margaret Fisher
Dana Graham
Abigail Jungreis
Christine Rogers
Harold Rosenberg
Kirk Scattergood
Patricia Schrader
Bonnie Wood

1976
Martin Belsky
Lisa Bobbie Hughes
Bradford Johnson
Daniel Kozarsky
Faith Nathan
Susan Troemner

1977
Denise Cosby
Jane Elkis
Karen Kozarsky
Pamela Greenberg
Toby Snider
Anne Widerstrom

1978
Judy Berman
Adam Belsky
Elise Feyerherm
Charles Krueger
Donald Leatherwood
Diane McAfoos
John Possumato
Lawrence Riesenbach

1979
Miriam Carrasquillo
Peter Greenberg
Judith Hartman
Diane Lees

1980
Gordon Beckhart
Mary Jo Coll
Joann Easling

Laura Hohnhold
Walter E. Hopton
Grant Lippincott
Robert Riesenbach
Dina Rudolph
Andrew Searle
Maria Serrano

1981
Joel Feyerherm
Jeanne Hauch
James Krueger
Nancy Loughridge
Robin Maurer
Elisa Urbanelli

1982
Vincent Cebula
Jonathan Dunn
Sheri Kapel
Marcela McAllister
Blake Moore
Anna Spruill
Frederick Young

1983
David Cebula
Eileen McAllister
Brian Mendelsohn

1984
Robin Bachin
Karin Bagnall
Gregory Billings
Rachel Boyce
James Buckwalter
Andrew Kociuba
Kerry Lippincott
Michael Rudolph
Scott Smith
Karen Stevenson

1985
Elizabeth Ahrens
Eric Boehme
Homer Cepeda
Elizabeth Geib
George Hart
Chong Dae Kim
Anne Lippincott
John Schnyder
Thomas Tatlow
David Williams

1986
Mark Buckwalter
Nicole Edmund
Joan Hohweiler
David Jefferds
Mark Mitchell
Robert Pineda
Verna Polutan
Amy Weeks
Tracey Whitesell

1987
Anne Blood
Sheila Cepeda

Daan Gilad
Chong Hwam Kim
Kimberly Lennox
Mansoor Movaghar
Marissa Ventura
Kirsten Wallenstein

1988
Steven Canfield
Tracy Gartmann
Barbara Johnson
Janice Johnston
Geraldine Nogaki
Nancy Polutan
Alice Roberts
Janet Vincent

1989
Bindiya Ananthakrishnan
Jennifer Ansel
Katherine Barnes
David Caparrelli
David Latterman

1990
Jennifer Boothby
Timothy Dreby
Min Jung Kang
James Muldowney

1991
Rebecca Ansel
Julian Austin
Victoria Bowden
Chad Brown
Colleen Coleman
Rajeeb Guharoy
Donald Orth
Rachel Williams
David Willison
Jocelyn Ziemian

1992
Susan Blood
Carla Cicalese
Daniel Diamond
Daniel Lutz
Annemarie Orth
Amrita Prabhakar

1993
Sonia Ananthakrishnan
Benjamin Boothby
Danielle DeCou
Erica Levin
Rachel Merkt
Suzanne Moeller
Jenny Sung-Sin Park
Aimee Penna

1994
Jesse Armiger
Joanna Dreby
Marisa Edmund
Nathaniel Evans
Tamika Harris
Maria Jose

1995
Ian Alteveer
David Baiada
Kelley Joy
Courtney Morris
Simona Munson
Jennifer Polutan
Julie Son
Judith Wallner

1996
Sarah Adelman
Aisha Barbour
Wilbur Briones
Stephen Cipolone
Kelli Markelwitz
Anastasia Pozdniakova

1997
Durell Bouchard
Robert Conde
Esther Horowitz
Nathaniel James

1998
Janice Baiada
Emina Imsirovic
Sadie Lang
Charles McNally
Sean Meckley
Selen Okcuoglu
Steven Porter
Tracy Ransome
Courtney Shipon
Mia Steinberg
Steven Van Name

1999
Palav Barbaria
Michael Brotzman
Peter Dempsey
Angela Dixon
Diana Geseking
Natasha Mitra
Imani Pearson
Loren Seaton
Mitesh Trivedi

2000
Heather Croshaw
Blair Dickinson
Olukemi Fajolu
Meruka Gupta
Brent Harrison
Timothy Kreider
Kevin Lee
Melissa Maquilan
Kari Myers
Alicia Resnick

2001
Jordan Barbour
Nadja Beglerovic
Frederick Bidrawn
Kara Duffy
Lawrence Henderson
Ryan McGee

Sara Nicolette
Rebecca Overholt
Akshay Sudhindra

2002
Elon Brown
Margaret Gentile
Grace Emiko Guthe
Kellie Machlus
Genevieve Maquilan
Gregory Mole
Aaron Moore
Clark Smith

2003
Tristan Bresnen
Deborah Harris
Jennifer McWilliams
Karalina Pulz
Mark Schenkel
Magan Sethi
Shang-Jui Wang
Christine Yankowski

2004
Jason Brody
Emily Einhorn
Julianne Eubank
Naomi Harper
Jamal Jones
Kalisa Martin
Julia Onorato
Julia Poszmik
Elizabeth Sabel
Alex Schank

2005
Sean DiStefano
Rebecca Gildiner
Gregory Guthe
Lisa Hummel
Katherine Kellom
Elyse Muratore
Lauren Nigro
Melanie Preston
Christine Schantz
Mankaran Singh
Christopher Yingling

2006
Ashley Alter
Caitlin Baiada
Allison Bernard
Danielle Chung
David Fischer
Nathan Harper
Benjamin Jones
Edward Kreider
Ryan Mulligan
Nina Schuchman
Benjamin Spielberg
Alexandra Stark

2007
David Bankes
Andrew Bernard
Sanjay Bhatt

Courtney Brown
Anthony Cordisco
Laurien Gilbert
Jennielle Jobson
Alexander Levy
Danielle Lynn
Kyle Nocho
David Sheffield
Tara Thomas
Sarah Van Cleve
Nadia Washlick

2008
Kira Adams
Ashley Edwards
Charles Hodgens
Emily Jones
Shaina Karasin
Samantha Kriger
Julie Martin
Rachel Mulligan
Andrea Onorato
Richard Rinaldi
Sarah Rosenbach
Kevin Schlagle
Eric Teitelbaum

2009
Kelly Barna
Orysia Bezpalko
Janak Bhatt
Aubrie Campbell
Sarah Connell
Sophia Demuynck
Russell Hensley
Hannah Levy
Hayden Moskowitz
Rebecca Salowe
Nina Samuel
Hannah Spielberg
Katie Stutz

2010
Emma Baiada
Alison Barton
Alissa Beckett
Monica Chelius
Phillip Dorsey
Robert Engel
Clara Fischer
Keyanah Freeland
Eric Maertin
Jacob Montgomery
Heather Moore
Kathryn Schlechtweg
Arianne Taormina
Tej Trivedi

2011 (inducted May 2010)
Peter Barna
Alleanna Harris
Isaias Muñoz
Samantha Saludades
Darshak Thosani
Brian White
David White

SCHOOL COMMITTEE

The School Committee, or Board of Trustees, includes up to 21 members, a majority of whom must be members of the Religious Society of Friends (Quakers). Members of the School Committee donate a considerable amount of time, financial support, and interest to guiding the affairs of the school. The overall and ultimate responsibility for school management and policies lies with the School Committee. Below are School Committee members who have served from 1920 to the present.

Anne Z. Conrow 1927–1932
Frances G. Conrow 1945–1951
Marguerite S. Cooper 1927–1942
Robert Cope 1992–1994
Josephine H. B. Copithorne 1951–1956
Esther L. Coriell 1969–1973
Sandra Croshaw 2004–2009
Thomas P. Darlington 1973–1977
Anna M. Darnell 1920–1922
Helen W. Darnell 1924–1925, 1926–1927
Marguerite C. Darnell 1968–1974
Charles F. Deaterly 1973–1975
Hannah E. S. DeCou 1931–1935
Howard F. DeCou 1920–1936
Richard T. DeCou 1972–1979
Samuel C. DeCou 1941–1942, 1945–1967
Thomas S. DeCou 1958–1974, 1986–1987
Wilda DeCou 1992–1995
Joanne DeLuca 1988–1989
Ellen DiPiazza 1983–1990
Smith E. Doane Jr. 1959–1967
Cynthia Dolbec 1997–2001
Meridee Duddleston .2005–
Anna B. Dudley 1920–1929
Levi L. Dudley 1920–1921
Nicole Edmund 2002–2004
Edith Edmunds 1979–1985
Thomas W. Elkinton .1930–1942
David Emmons 2000–2007
Arthur H. Evans 1945–1959, 1963–1974
Lois M. Evans 1969–1970
Robert T. Evans 1920–1921
Elissa Favata 2000–2004
Susanna Ford 1981–1985
Mary Forsythe 1953–1970, 1971–1979
H. Lindley Gardiner Jr. 1964–1970
Laura W. Gaskill 1956–1970
Elizabeth L. Gillingham 1945–1961
Jan Gillespie 1995–1997
Robert W. Gray 1977–1984
David D. Griscom 1936–1942
Helen T. Griscom 1941–1942, 1945–1950
J. Milton Griscom 1930–1941
Renu Gupta 1997–2001
William Guthe 1984–1998, 2001–
C. William Haines Jr. .1963–1971
Charlotte E. Haines 1920–1924
Elizabeth M. Haines .1951–1979
Ella Haines 1964–1970
Lenore B. Haines 1945–1971
Samuel S. Haines 1920–1930
Sara W. Haines 1938–1942
Noel Harbist 1996–2005
Marion W. Harmer 1920–1934
Edward S. Harmer 1920–1926
David C. Harris 2004–
Ellen Wolf Harris 1998–2004
Joseph Harris 1993–2002
Diana L. Harrison 1968–1983
Neil Hartman 1997–2005
Katharine T. Haupt 1968–1989
Michael Hayes 1994–1999
W. Waldo Hayes 1927–1932

W. Harold Heritage 1969–1971
A. Clark Hobbie Jr. 1971–1979
Laurie Hodian 2002–2010
Elwood Hollingshead 1920–1937,
1938–1939, 1957–1959
Irving Hollingshead 1937–1938, 1938–1942,
1945–1957, 1959–1968
George L. Holmes 1920–1921
Pattie Hopton 1976–1982
Edward Hovatter 2002–
James D. Hull Jr. 1957–1964, 1986–1988
Jackie James 1984–1988
Florence E. Jefferis 1935–1942, 1945–1950
Betsy Harman Johnson 1975–1985, 1987–1992
Floyd Johnson 2000–2003
Nancy Jones 1978–1980
Margaret E. Jones 1929–1930, 1959–1968
John Kavanaugh 1949–1953
Louise Wright Khanlian 2007–
John F. Kincaid 1953–1954
Steven King 1991–1997
Barbara Kirschner 1979–1984
Ann McV. Knight 1955–1956
Peter J. Koblenzer 1964–1967
Cheryl Kozloff 1990–1999
Robert Kreider 1994–1998
Jean Landis 1973–1984
John Langel 1990–1998
Suzanne Lankenau 1983–1991
John Latimer 2009–
Ann Lenhart 1976–1977
Mary Liddle 1978–1981
Morris Linton 1921–1926
M. Albert Linton 1920–1942, 1945–1966
Marion L. Linton 1932–1935
William H. Linton 1927–1935
David R. Lippincott 1920–1938
Philip Lippincott 2010–
Alice Martin 1977–1979
Lucile Mason 1959–1962
Anne Matlack 1996–1999, 2000–2005
Louis R. Matlack 1970–
Marian J. Matlack 1923–1942, 1945–1946
Marion S. Matlack 1920–1923
Robert W. Matlack 1945–1962
Samuel R. Matlack 1920–1942
Daniel E. Maxfield 1920–1922
Stephen W. Meader 1929–1942
Mary Louise Melchior 1965–1972
Arthur Mendelsohn 1981–1987
Carolyn Miller 1976–1991
Mark Mitchell 2005–
John F. Moore 1981–1987
Caroline Moriuchi 1984–1996
Fred T. Moriuchi 1971–1995
Naoji Moriuchi 2005–
Takashi Moriuchi 1956–1988, 1989–
Dryden P. Morse 1966–1972
Charles Mulloy Jr. 1955–1958
Elizabeth D. Mutch 1966–1969
Rebecca McIlvain 1955–1956
Jack McKeon 1983–1993
John E. McVaugh Jr. 1962–1973

Schelysture McWhorter 1984–1989
Rex McWilliams 1998–2004
Charlotte D. Nelson 1970–1973,
1986–1990, 1998–2001
Eliza S. Nicholson 1920–1936
John W. Nicholson .1960–1965
Kathry Russell Nissen 1979–1982
Mary Noland 1998–2001
Elizabeth Jayne Oasin 1991–1995
Judith Obbard 1983–1990
Peter Obbard 1997–2000
Donald Orth 1990–1997
Pauline Shaw Pennington 1981–1988
Alice S. Perkins 1920–1942, 1945–1948
E. Russell Perkins .1926–1942
Elizabeth H. Pfaffmann 1973–1975
Lindley B. Reagan 1954–1963, 1965–1969
Gretchen Van Meter Rector 1981–1984
Sandra H. Reid 1982–1986
Grace E. Rhoads 1920–1922
Richard H. Rhoads 1945–1956
William E. Rhoads .1920–1929
Elliott Richardson .1983–1988
Anna B. S. Richie 1920–1927
Edward L. Richie 1920–1922
Eleanor S. Richie 1956–1958
Mary Richie 1975–1977
Paul Riggins 1999–2009
Barbara Ritson 1985–1986
David Robbins 1975–1979
Lewis M. Robbins .1973–1974
Alice L. Roberts 1950–1953
Anna C. Roberts 1922–1940
Harvey M. Roberts 1922–1927
Horace Roberts 1923–1931
Lydia L. Roberts 1934–1942, 1945–1946
Malcolm H. Roberts 1950–1988
Margaret Roberts .1978–1990
Marian C. Roberts 1920–1942, 1945–1949
Preston T. Roberts 1922–1942
Wm. H. Roberts Jr. 1926–1942, 1945–1953
Vincent L. Robertson 1979–1989
Henry Robinson 1984–1988
Anne W. Rogers 1925–1942, 1945–1947
Joseph E. Rogers .1946–1963
Robert J. Rogers 1935–1942, 1945–1953
Elizabeth S. Russell 1934–1937
Theresa O. Russell 1963–1965
Thomas K. Russell 1972–1978
Ruth Sawyer 1978–1981
Warren Sawyer 1982–1988
Henry W. Schilling 1975–1978
William N. Schultz 1989–1995
Robert W. Scott 1956–1970
Thomas Sedlacek .1998–2000
Dan Seeger 2005–
Ruth M. Sharpless 1932–1942, 1945–1947
Susan E. Sharpless 1920–1922
David Smith 1995–1998
Drew Smith 2003–
Eleanor S. Smith .1945–1948
Howard Christopher Smith 1985–1986
Doris L. Sowton 1956–1964

Susan E. W. Spencer 1926–1932
Kathryn C. Stackhouse 1950–1963
Thomas Stackhouse 1996–2002
Nancy J. Stickney .1970–1973
Caroline Stiles 1920–1929
Agnes N. Stokes 1936–1942, 1945–1951
Francis C. Stokes Jr. 1960–1972
Mary Emlen Stokes 1920–1926
Joseph Stokes 1920–1942
Lydia B. Stokes 1973–1978
S. Emlen Stokes 1926–1942, 1945–1973
Deborah F. Stratton 1922–1934
May R. Taylor 1945–1951
Sylvia E. Taylor 1967–1973, 1994–1997
Janet Sawyer Thomas 1991–1996, 1997–2000
Frances M. Thorne 1922–1942, 1945–1946
Nathan Thorne 1920–1930, 1931–1941
Susan Tracey 1999–2006
Laurence Van Meter 1992–1994
Margaret M. Van Meter 1952–1969
Joseph A. Vlaskamp 1974–1976
Henry R. Walton .1931–1940
Carol W. Walz 1995–2003
Miriam C. Ward 1961–1970
William H. Watson 1972–1975
Deborah Whitesell 1990–1995
Hannah D. Wildman 1951–1980
William E. Wilkins 1953–1964
Emily Williams 1970–1974
Rena M. Williams .1953–1966
James Wilson 1975–1984
Robert E. Wilson 1953–1959, 1965–1970
Patricia Wilus 2001–2004
William T. Wohlford 1970–1972
Irvina W. Wolfe 1945–1949
Alexander C. Wood Jr. 1922–1942, 1945–1953
Alexander C. Wood III 1953–1963
George D. Wood 1945–1949
Gertrude S. E. Wood 1927–1942
Helen C. Wood 1932–1942, 1945–1968
James A. E. Wood .1963–1978
Nancy M. Wood 1940–1942, 1945–1952
Richard R. Wood 1954–1956
Harold K. Wright Sr. 1952–1972,
1985–1992, 1993–2002
Cindy Yingling 1995–2005, 2006–2009
Stephanie Zarus 2008–
Kenneth Zekavat 1995–2004, 2005–
Thomas Zemaitis .1992–2003

INDEX

Numbers in *italics* indicate photographs.

A

A Better Chance (ABC), 61
Acme building, 50
Adelman, Sarah Wallace, 114–15
Advanced Placement courses, 50, 70, 74–76, 110
Affiliation Program, 96
Alice Paul Merit Award, 114, 121
Allen, Sam, 22, 24
Alley, Donna, 77
All-School Picnic, 100, *101*
alumni, involvement of, 114–15
Alumni Association, 114
Alumni Association awards, 121
Alumni Weekend, 104, *110*
American Friends Service Committee, 96, 97, 98
Archer, William R., 102
archery, *31*
Armstrong, Harley, *78*, 81
arts, as part of Moorestown Friends School
    education, 66, 67, 73, *74*, 76, 86,
    87–89, 100
Arts Center, 46, 112, 113
art show, *77*, 86
athletic fields, *8*, *11*, *29*
athletics, 67, 72. *See also* archery, lacrosse,
    soccer, tennis
Avery, Mary Ellen, 105

B

Baiada, Anne, *112*
Baiada, Caitlin, *112*
Baiada, Diane, 112–13
Baiada, Emma, *112*
Baiada, Mark, *46*
Baiada, Mel, 112–13
Baiada family, 112
Baldwin, Anne, *78*
Barrett, Ruth Stephen, *99*
Barrett, W. Elmer, 11, 22–24
Bartley, Frances, *78*
Basch, Peter, 97
Bayshore Discovery Project, *72*
Beck, Maggie Ritchie, *75*
Bhatt, Sanjay, 102
Bicentennial Celebration, 39–41, 105
Big Old Gym (B.O.G.), 100
Blackburn, Grace Kennedy, 54, 97
Blatherwick, Chuck, *73*
Blood, Anne, 89
Bonder, Jim, 105
Borton, Allis, 51
Bottomer, Jim, 108
Boyer, Doug, *50*
Brandimarto, Larry, 45
Brick, Lynne D., 51, 54, 113–14
bricklaying, 103
Bridge, Gardiner, *41*, 42
Brudon, Florence "Floss," 29, 38, 51, 82–83, 84,
    102, 108
Bryen, Brad, *36*
Bursch, Dee, 100
Bushnell, Elizabeth, *78*

C

Cadbury family, 28
Caldwell, Barbara, 61, *69*, 76–77
Calta, Daan (Ze'ev Gilad), 70
Camden Scholars Program, 60, 61–62, *63*, 92
Campaign for Arts, Athletics, and Endowment,
    46, 112–13
Campaign 2000, 46
Camp Bernie, *49*, 96, *104*
Camp Dark Waters, 96
capital campaigns, 38, 46, 112–13
Capstone project, 74
Carr, Wilbur E. "Toddy," 25, 69, *78*, 80, 81
Casne, Debra Muzyka, *66*
Caughey, John, 84, 97, 109, 117–18
Chester Preparative Meeting of Friends, 14,
    15, 109
Chester Reagan Chair in Faith and Practice, 38,
    46, 59, 76, 117
Chestertown (NJ), 14
City Project, 70, 85
Clarke, Tim, 66
class trips, 96. *See also* field trips
Clauss, Beth Freeland, 102
clubs, 61, 73, *99*
Cobbs, Sam, 96, 97
Coles, Marshall, 88
Coles, William C., Jr., 80
Color Day, 47, 105
community service, 55–56, 67, 72
Coney, Gwendolyn, *78*
Corsey, Tina Wheaton, 62, *76*
Cowan, Marguerite C., *78*, *99*, 105
Cowperthwaite, Ann, 16
Cowperthwaite, Job, 16
Cox, Archibald, *36*
Craig, Alan R., 43–47, 50, 109, 110
Craig, Mary, 45
Cranford (1923), *20*
Cum Laude Society, 121
Cupola (1970), *45*

D

Darlington, LeRoy, *78*
Darnell, Peggy Cooper, 66
Davis, Linsey, 73
Dawson, Marge, 93, 101
DeCou, George, 16
DeCou, Tom, 59
DeCou family, 28, 112
DeKlyn, Marjorie, *78*
Delamater, Jerry, 97
Denworth, Katharine M., 23
Deyo, Alfred L., 23, *78*, 80–81
Diller, Bill, *115*
Diller family, 112
Diller Library renovation, 112
DiMaggio, Paul, *99*
Dining Hall Commons, *45*, 46, *47*, 55, 112
Dinner Among Friends, 104, *115*
diversity, 91, 110
    commitment to, 59, 60–62
    increasing, for staff and students, 50
    Moorestown Friends School's embracing
        of, 92
    in today's student body, 51
Diversity Committee, 61
Dreby, Ed, 85
Durbin, Dorothy, 67

E

Edmund, Genevieve, 88
Edmund, Gwynne, 88
Edmund, Marisa, 88
Edmund, Nicole, 88
Edmund, Robert, 88
Edmund Optics, 111
Edmunds, Henry, *78*
Edwards, Ashley, *72*
Edwards, Hazel, 93, 101
elementary school, *30*, 33
Endowment for Faculty Support, 46
endowment for Quaker education, 112
Eni family, 112
Ensemble, 87–88, 89
Evesham Monthly Meeting, 14
Examined Life program, 9, 50, 62
exchange programs, 34, 67, 96–98

F

faculty
    authority of, 33, 42
    fall faculty tea, 29
    meetings of, 45
    salaries of, 33, 50, 110
Field House, 46, 112, 113
field trips, 36, 70, 73, 96
financial aid, 36, 110
Fox, George, 9, 120
Franklin, Benjamin, 79
Freeland, Beth Clauss, 59
Friends Council on Education (FCE), 116
Friends' High School, 18–19, 56–58
    faculty and school committee (1886), *106*
    merger of, with Moorestown Friends'
        Academy, 12, 13, 19
Friendship Fair, 47, 99, *99*
Friends schools. *See also* Quaker education
    issues facing, 116
    mission of, 53
    Quaker values at, 48
Frola, Rose, 107
Funny Girl, 98

G

Geary, Louise Morgan, 100
Goin' Buggy, 76
Gornto, Mark, 100, 108
Goula, Kelly, 68
Grandparents' Day, *102*, 103
Green, Leonard, 105
Greenleaf Retirement Community property,
    50, 118
Guthe, Geoffrey "Yas," *113*
Guthe, William, 45–46, 111–12, *113*
Guzman, Sonia Mixter, 108

H

Hadley, Genevieve, *78*
Haines, Ephraim, 15
Hansen, Christopher, 68
Harris, David C., 74
Hartman, Neil, 29, 33, 51, 69, 83, 84, 85–87, 96
Heath, Sandy, 51, 84, 85, 119
Henry, Carol, 39
Hensley, Russell, 66
Hersperger, Helen, *78*
Hiatt, Merrill L., 30–34
Hicksite Friends, 18
Hicksite Meeting (Moorestown, NJ), 13, 19, 22

high school, opening of, 25–27
Hippo, the, *100*, 101
Hoagies with the Head, *49*
Honors Program, 50, 70–72, 74–76, 110
Howard, Brian, 107
Hughes, Lisa Bobbie Schreiber, 105
Hull, Deborah Miller, 82
Hull, T. Reagan, 29
Hurricane Katrina, charitable support for victims of, 111

I

independent schools, teaching ethics and morality, 118
Intensive Learning program, 36, 39, 70, 72, 73, 85, 104
Irwin, Mrs. Barbara, 105

J

Jacob, Louisa M., 80
Jenkins, Tiffany Taylor, 60
John, Carolyn A., 80
Joseph and the Amazing Technicolor Dreamcoat, 107–8

K

Kaiser, Claire, 90
Kaiser, Teri, 68, 89–90
Kean, Thomas, 41
Kelly, Maeve, 67, 74
Khan, Mustapha, *99*, 109
Kimberly, Chris, 70
King, Martin Luther, Jr., 86
Kingston, William H., III, 17, 19, 116
Kleiner, Carolyn, *99*
Kotlikoff, Larry, 97
Kozloff, Cheryl, 58
Kozloff, Chick, 58
Kozloff, Kacy, 58
Kreider, Barbara, *92*, 93, 120
Kreider, Tim, 77, *99*
Kucinich, Dennis, 103

L

lacrosse, 38, *83*, *108*
Laufenberg, George, 86
LaVia, John "Doc," *99*
Lawson, Blanche, 97
Lawson, Louise, 97
Lehfeldt, Martin C., 105
library, *32*, *85*, 112
Lippincott, Joseph, *78*
Lippincott, Naomi, 37
Lippincott, Philip, 37
Lippincott family, 96
Lloyd, Chris, 104
Lobster Dinner, 104
Lojek, Chris, *50*
Lower School, *7*, *33*, 68–69
Lower School Art Show, 86

M

MacColl, Alexander M., 35–42, 48, 50, 59, 85
Magee, Herman M., 25, 28, 29, 51, *78*, 80, 81–82, 85
Main Street, *10*, 98
Mansfield, Margaret Barnes, 85, 86
Marcucci, Richard, 65–66, 88–89, 98, 100
Martin, Lisa Thomas, 54, 120
Martin Luther King Jr. Day of Service, *114*
Matlack, Louis R., 36–37, 44, 59 112

Matlack, Robert, 24
Matlack, William, 16
Matlack family, 28, 112
May Day, 47, 86, 96, *97*
McEwan, Patricia, *71*, 110
McKeon, Jack, 44
Meader, Helen, *78*
Mecray, Paul, 81
Meeting House, 51, 54–55
Meeting for Worship, 50, 54–55, 62, 86, 95, 105, 117–18
Metzer, Pat, 114
MFS Artist-in-Residence, 37
MFS-Camden Community Scholarship Program, 36, 37
Middle School, 69–70
Miller, George Macculloch "Cully," 29, 34, 38, 51, *78*, 81, 82, 84–85
Mitchell, Mark, 63, *111*, 120
Mock Political Convention, 34, *36*, 84, 85, 92, *94*, 99, 102
Mock Primary Election, 102, 103
Moore, Thomas, 14
Moorestown (NJ)
    changes in, 119
    declining number of Quakers in, 19, 58–59
    first kindergarten class in, 18
    history of, 14
    Main Street, *10*, 98
    public schools in, 30
Moorestown Friends' Academy, *13*, 18–19, 58
    1880 student body, *18*
    expansion of 17–18
    kindergarten (1898), *16*
    merger of, with Friends' High School, 12, 13, 19
    purchase of land for, 15
    stone schoolhouse of, 15–16, *19*
Moorestown Friends Meeting, schools organized by, 16–17
Moorestown Friends School
    admissions, increasing standards for, 45
    aerial view, *21*, *116*
    annual giving campaigns, 38
    becoming a more democratic institution, 38
    Bicentennial Celebration, 39–41, 105
    building campaigns, 25–27, 32, 33
    capital campaigns, 38, 46, 112–13
    creation of, 19
    diversity commitment at, 60–62, 92
    early history of, 13–19
    educational approach at, 54–59, 65–77
    enrollment at, 24, 30–32, 35, 36, 41–42, 45, 119
    expansion of, 25–27
    financial difficulties at, 42–43
    first day of kindergarten at, 14
    first years of, 22–24
    future of, 116–20
    growing number of non-Quaker families at, 30
    heads of school, 20–51
    marketing campaign, 65
    mission statement of, 34, 52–54
    1948 faculty of, *78*
    opening of, 11–13
    Quaker approach to education at, 54–59
    rebuilding curriculum at, 42
    reinforcing Quaker culture at, 62–63
    rising financial aid budget at, 62
    scholastic standards of, 29, 45

school colors of, 24
shrinking numbers of Quakers at, 58–59
social and political upheaval at (1960s–70s), 35–37, 39
strategic plan (1970s), 37
strategic plan (2004), 50, 62, 70, 110
teachers and coaches at, 79–93
traditions at, 94–105
young students at (1929), *26*
Moorestown and Her Neighbors (DeCou), 16
Moorestown Meeting, split of, 13
Moorestown Meeting House, 14
Moorestown Monthly Meeting, 109
Moorestown's Third Century: The Quaker Legacy (Kingston), 17
Moose, Rob, 102
Moriuchi, Carol "Kiyo," 62, 102, 107, *113*
Moriuchi, Fred T., 43–44
Moriuchi, Takashi "Tak," 59, 97–98
Moriuchi, Yuri, 97–98
Moriuchi family, 45, 96, 97–98, 112
Movaghar, Mansoor, 70
Muldowney, James A. S., III, 105
music
    Ensemble, 87–88, 89
    not taught in early Friends' schools, 12
    Suzuki violin instruction, *68*, 93, 101
Mystic Seaport (CT), 36, 70, 96, *105*

N

nature walks, 96
New Gym, 100
New Jersey, public schools in, 17

O

Oliver, Norman, 112
Oliviero, Beth, 100
Oliviero, Jamie, 105
Omilian, Michael, 77, 90, 91, 105
Orthodox Meeting (Moorestown, NJ), 13, 19, 22

P

Pages Lane, 112
parents, involvement of, 113–14
Paul, Alice, 18, 118
Perez, Erick, *54*
Philadelphia Weekend Work Camp, 100
Phillips, Polly, *78*
physical education program, *99*
Pope, Alexander, 29
Porter, Steven, 62
Price, Harrie B., III, 25, 28, 29, 51, 84, 104, 105
prom, 29, 98
property, purchase of, 110, 118
public schools, 30, 96
Purdy, James, 119

Q

Quaker Breakfast, 103
Quaker education
    effect on, of school size, 119
    goal of, 9
    prevalence of, 14
    values of, 117
Quakerism
    influence of, on school's programs, 34
    teaching of, at Moorestown Friends School, 54–59
Quaker Ladies, 46, 54
Quakers
    beliefs of, 12

diminishing numbers of, 19, 116–17
educational approach of, 56–58
excellence and, 76
Quinn, Ted, *58*

R

Ransome, Whitty, 102
Rate Bill schools, 17
Rats! 76
Reagan, Chester L., 24–30, 33, 51, *78*, 80, 81
Reagan, Peter, 110
Red and Blue, 25, 29
Red Gym, 100
Red Sock Run, *107*
religious education, 34, 59
Religious Life Committee, 58
Rencewicz, Michael, 102
Richie, David S., 25, 66, 81, 100
Richter, Emma, 101
Ricketts, Jean, 51, 81, 100
Roberts, Joshua, 15
Roberts family, 28
Roberts Hall, 27
Robotics program, 74
Rodmantown (NJ), 14
Rosenberg, Anne, 105
Rosenberg, Joan, *38*
Rudolf Steiner School (Nürnberg, Germany), 97

S

Salowe, Rebecca, 65
Sawyer, Ruth, 84
School Committee, 109–12, 123
    Craig nurturing relationships with, 46
    dealing with issues after MacColl's
        resignation, 42
    keeping school afloat during Depression and
        World War II, 28
    pushing Barrett to become first headmaster,
        22–23
    reinforcing Quaker culture at Moorestown
        Friends School, 62–63
school size, 119
Schopfel, Brent, 103
Scripture classes, 59
SEED (Seeking Educational Equity and Diversity),
    61, 92
senior benches, 98
senior play, 29
senior privileges, 98
Senior Projects, 36
Service Award, 114, 121
service learning program, 59
Shaffer, Steve, *73*
Shannon, Mary McVaugh, 84
Sharpless family, 28
Shelley, Warren, Jr., 67, 84
Smith, Ben "Buck," 107
Smith, Robert, 53, 100
soccer, 38, *82*, 115
Social Security Dances, 98
Spielberg, Ben, 103
Spirit Week, 101
sports. *See* athletics
Spring Parents Auction, 37
Starr, Victoria, 84
Stevens, Janet N., 38–39
Stiles, Mrs. Marion, 102
Stokes, Lydia, 59, 112
Stokes, Sally, *78*
Stokes family, 28, 112
Stokes Forest (NJ), 70, *73*, *97*

Stokes Hall, 41, 42, 53, 112
stone schoolhouse, 15–16, *19*, *30*
Stouffer, Richard, 88
student government, 25, 59
Suzuki violin instruction, *68*, 93, 101
Swan, Martha C. H., 23, 80

T

Tate, Kathy, 107
Taylor, Harold E., *99*
Taylor, Jim, 85
Taylor, Joe, Jr., 69, 87
Taylor, May Roberts, 17
Taylor, Robert M., 25, *78*, 80, 99
Taylor-Williams, Priscilla, 54, 63, 89, *119*
teachers. *See* faculty
technology, 59, 91
    school's first computer, 86
    used in teaching, 85
tennis, *24*, 86
Thanksgiving Happening, *102*, 103
theater program, 73, 100, 107–8
Thomas, George, 104
Thomas, Janet Sawyer, 83, *99*

U

Upper School, *9*, 70–77
Urbanelli, Elisa, 102

V

Van Meter, Laurence R. (Larry), 47–51, 77, 83,
    116–20
Van Meter, Luke, *48*
Van Meter, Margaret, *48*
Van Meter, Matty, *48*
Vietnam War, protest against, 86

W

Washington, Karen, 55, 60, 91–92, 120
weighty Quakers, 46. *See also* School Committee
Weiner, Davie, 51, 87–88, 89
West Building, 33, *34*, 46
West Meeting House, *17*, 25
White Building, 25, *36*
Whitfield, Kendra, 66
Wilkins, Clinton P., 42
Williams, Mary, 62
Williams, Ruth Conrow, 80
Wilson, Doris, 108
Wilson, Helen, 12
Wolf, Lindsay, 98
Wood, Anne, 67, 102
Wood, Elizabeth Cooper, 66, *99*
wooden tennis courts, *24*
Wood family, 97
Woodson, Cornell, 101, 102, 120
World War II, challenges of, 28–29

Y

Yingling, Christopher, 120
Yingling, Cynthia Eni (Cindy), *46*, 120
Yingling, Gregory, 120
Yingling, Timothy, 120
Yingling family, 112
Young, Elizabeth, *112*
Young, Joseph, *112*
Young Alumni Award, 114–15, 121

Z

Zekavat, Kenneth, 56, 115
Zemaitis, Jacqueline, 66
Zemaitis, Thomas E., 43, 109–10